Vol. III

By Cassie Wild and M.S. Parker

Published by Belmonte Publishing.

ISBN-13: 978-1514192368

ISBN-10: 1514192365

Table of Contents

Chapter 1

Aleena

The wind cut into me as I bent over the railing of Bank Rock Bridge to stare into the water. It was cold, icy and sharp, but it was nothing compared to the misery I felt inside.

Sleeping with the help.

If I thought it would lessen the pain, I'd have made myself puke, just to get rid of all the poison that seemed to choke me. But it wouldn't do any good. This kind of pain didn't come from anything physical.

I could still see the look of disdain she'd given me—and the complete and utter withdrawal on Dominic's face as he watched.

He hadn't said *anything*.

Logically, I knew it was possible to hurt like this.

Logically, I should have already been *prepared* for something like this. I'd been in this position before after all.

Danny Holton hadn't pretended to care about me the way Dominic had though. Dominic had made think he...

"What?" I muttered to myself. A few feet away, a couple with a camera looked at me oddly.

Tourists, no doubt about it. New Yorkers were used to people talking to themselves—or to a street post or the clear blue air. Then, to my surprise, I was able to laugh at myself, even if only inside my head. After a little more than six months, I was already feeling like a New Yorker.

Although sometimes, like now, I hated it here. My laughter faded away.

The couple was still watching me and I managed to give them a weak smile. They hurried off and I went back to staring down into the water. It rippled slightly in the wind, casting back a wavering reflection.

Made you think what? I asked my unsteady double down in the water. *Made you think he cared?*

Sure he did. He cared. In an abstract sort of way. He wasn't a complete asshole like Gary. But he didn't *really* care. He might like me on a casual level, but in the end, what mattered was the fact that I was handy. Easy access to a piece of ass. Easy access to an *agreeable* piece of ass too. My face flushed all the way to my ears. I'd been naïve. He liked to play kinky games and I'd been open to learning.

It was as simple as that.

I'd been stupid enough to think otherwise.

I'd *wanted* to think otherwise.

But if I'd mattered...

I sniffled and dashed at the tears on my face.

If I'd mattered, he wouldn't have let her talk to me like that.

Exotic. Somehow, that word was worse than some of the derogatory insults I'd experienced.

"I should have told her to wait a few minutes and I'd go find my servant girl uniform and get her some tea and crumpets," I muttered, dashing another tear away. "Just to see what she said."

At least I'd stood up to her. At least I'd *said* something. I hadn't been able to do that the last time people had torn me down.

And it was more than Dominic had done.

He'd just...sat there.

My heart twisted again and I shoved away from the railing. Starting to walk, I focused on the wide, winding sidewalks of Central Park. If I gazed up in a certain direction, I could see the penthouse, so I didn't let myself look, not until the trees and paths hid it from view. Then it was almost like being back in Iowa, and right now, that was comforting.

It was cold and my legs had long since gone numb, but the last thing I wanted to do was go back to the penthouse. I didn't feel comfortable calling it *home.*

It *wasn't* home. I wasn't even sure I wanted it to be home. Not *now.*

With a knot choking me, I swiped at the tears burning a path down my face. I ended up bumping into a woman—she was dressed for exercise and she waved off my apology, clearly into her power-walk. All around me, people moved with purposes, even those who were just out to get their calorie burn on. I was just here to...

I stopped in the middle of the path.

I didn't *know* why I was here.

Other than to get away from Dominic.

He'd just sat there, staring at his mother. He'd barely even *looked* at me.

Sleeping with the help...

But that's what I am.

Frustrated and hurting all over again, I stormed over to a bench and dropped down on it. She'd talked about me like I was next to nothing and he hadn't said a word.

Yeah, I was his employee, but he could have said something. He hadn't and that hurt was an ugly, vicious wound inside me. I didn't know how to handle it, how to process it. Forcing myself to swallow past the knot in my throat, I leaned back and stared out across the park, watching the people without really seeing them.

I'd messed up.

Being attracted to Dominic as I'd been, I hadn't let myself think things through and maybe that was understandable. It had put me where I was now and it wasn't a good place.

I'd slept with my boss.

Worse, I cared about him.

The question now was, what was I going to do?

I had absolutely no idea.

***

I found myself at Molly's.

Over the past few months, she'd become my best friend and there was little I couldn't tell her, but after she'd ushered me inside and put a hot cup of coffee in my frozen hands, I just shook my head.

"I wish you'd tell me what's wrong," she said, snuggled up on her ragged couch next to me. "I mean...I can guess it's about Dominic. We were just talking earlier, but now you look like he told you that fairytales aren't real."

"What?" I managed a wan smile in her direction. "You mean they're not? My Prince Charming isn't coming?" My heart gave a painful thump.

"He got lost on the way to the ball, that's all." She gave me an affectionate smile.

It was a familiar joke between us, but I couldn't make myself smile back at her this time.

Lifting my coffee to my lips, I sipped it. Its warmth was slowly seeping into my frozen hands and I thought that maybe, in a few more hours, they'd thaw out. "I just need to not think about it for a little while, Mol."

"I think you need to talk about it," she said, shaking her head. "You look terrible."

"Gee, thanks." I made a face at her. After one

more sip of coffee, I rested my head on the back of the couch and stared up at the ceiling. There was an old water stain that had been there since she'd moved in. It was vaguely Iowa-shaped and looking at it filled me with foreboding. “I’m just...tired.”

I wasn’t lying. My body ached in the best of ways and if it hadn’t been for the interruption, I wanted to think that I could, even now, be lying in bed with Dominic. Maybe we could have—

I shoved the thought away.

It was for the best that his mother had interrupted.

Now I knew what I was dealing with.

“I know that look on your face.”

I shot Molly a look and immediately wished I hadn’t. She had a shrewd, knowing look in her eyes and I could imagine her seeing straight through my skull, finding the memory of what had happened earlier...

And then hunting down Dominic Snow and punching him in the nose.

Molly wasn’t the sort of girl who had problems standing up to people. She could stand up for herself and her friends. It didn't matter that he was more than a foot taller and she weighed about a hundred pounds dripping wet.

Abruptly, I stood up, moving so fast the coffee sloshed out and burned my hand. “Ouch!” Bobbling the cup to keep from spilling more, I headed over to the tiny kitchen area. Her apartment was even smaller than the one I’d shared with Emma, but in

New York, that was to be expected. The eating, sleeping and living area was all in one area and if you're having company in this place, it better be somebody you liked. I dumped the coffee down the drain and stood there, taking a minute to calm my breathing and make sure I wasn't going to cry. It wouldn't help. It definitely wouldn't help.

"Do you mind if I just crash here for a while? I can sleep on the couch."

I turned and gave her my best smile, hoping she couldn't see how close I was to falling apart.

Molly was much better at being a friend than I was at acting. She gave me an easy smile and pretended not to notice how close I was to sobbing like a child. "Knock yourself out, Aleena. Just promise me you haven't started snoring."

Chapter 2

Dominic

Furious with both my mother and myself, I slammed the bedroom door and locked it, taking five seconds—just five—to turn the air blue before I grabbed a clean pair of jeans. After I dragged them on, I moved back out into the living room.

Ignoring my mother, I stared hard at the front door, almost willing it to open, but it didn't.

When it didn't, I stormed over and jerked it open, but the small hallway was empty.

Aleena was already gone.

Of course, the fact that she'd been pulling on her coat while I'd stood there like a statue should have been the first clue.

Swearing all over again, I came back in, not bothering to shut the door. Shoes...shoes...I saw my tennis shoes near the TV and shoved my feet in, sans socks. That was fine. Who needed socks?

My clothes were strewn on the floor, a clear sign of what we'd been doing when my mother decided to crash her way into my personal life—again. Snagging the steel gray dress shirt from the floor, I dragged it on and buttoned it. Now I had a shirt. Jeans, shirt, shoes. That covered it. And a coat because it was cold.

I jerked open the closet as my mother asked, "What are you doing, Dominic?"

"Going after Aleena."

"Whatever for?" she asked, clearly baffled.

I ignored the question.

It was harder to ignore her hand on my arm.

I tried to shake her off but Jacqueline St. James-Snow doesn't get *shaken* off. Her manicured hand didn't precisely tighten, but I felt it close like a shackle around me. "Really, Dominic. What were you thinking?"

"What was I thinking?" I demanded. It took all the control I had not to just let her have it. "Mother, I'll be honest—*thought* didn't come into the equation at the time."

She made a dismissive noise in her throat. "Don't be so crude."

Her hand fell away as I jammed my arms into my sleeves. I moved to the phone. I'd called downstairs, tell them to stop her. I could still catch her.

"Let her *go*, Dominic. Really. Please...sit. I came over here because we need to talk."

"Next time, call first," I suggested. I rubbed my hand over my chest. There was a dull ache there, one I wasn't familiar with.

Aleena was angry and hurt. She could probably use a few minutes to calm down.

Maybe...I blew out a breath.

Okay, I wasn't in the best frame of mind to talk to her and she was probably mad and hurt.

So I'd let her have a few minutes, then call her. We could meet somewhere and I'd buy her dinner. I could make this right. Aware that my mother was still watching, I looked over at her. "I don't want to talk to you right now. I'm pissed off at you."

"Because of that woman?" My mother waved a hand. "Dominic, she's hardly the first low-class girl I've caught you with. If you must bed them, so be it. But for it to be a girl you work with, it's not wise. She could cause you a great deal of trouble."

I waited until she was done. I even waited an extra few seconds, hoping it might calm the sharp edge of anger bubbling inside me. It didn't work.

"Low-class," I said, biting the words off. "That *low-class girl* is one of the sweetest, kindest women I've ever met. She doesn't sit around and plan about how she can use the connections she's made—"

"She doesn't *have* connections," Jacqueline said, laughing. "What kind of *connections* does a girl like that have?"

"Enough!" Slashing a hand through the air, I snapped, "I am *done* with this. I'm tired of it. To you, people with money are the superior species. But have you forgotten...*I was adopted*! For all *I* know, I came from that *low-class* group you so despise."

Jacqueline's face went tight, her mouth taking

on a pinched look. “Dominic, you are *my* son. That is all that matters.”

“It’s not all that matters to me!”

She stiffened, her face jerking back as though I’d slapped her. Slowly, like a queen rising from her throne, she came off the couch. “I see this isn’t the ideal time for us to talk.”

“What clued you in?”

She didn’t answer.

I stared at her rigid back as she walked to the door. She paused there momentarily as if expecting me to let her out...or apologize.

I stayed where I was.

After a few more seconds, she opened the door.

When it shut behind her, I moved into my bedroom. It was time to track down Aleena.

***

There was a problem with that idea and I figured it out less than ten minutes later.

Holding her cellphone in my hand, I slumped into the comfortable cushions of the couch and stared up at the ceiling.

She’d left her phone and I had no idea where she could have gone.

I’d slept with her twice now, had lived with her for weeks, and yet I knew so little about her. I knew the way her body responded to my touch. The way mine tightened every time she walked into the room. But I didn't know her.

What did she like to do?

Where would she go when she was upset?

I knew her friend's name was Molly and I knew where Molly worked, but...what else did I know?

Aleena was from Iowa.

The first and only other guy she'd slept with was a piece of shit.

And I'd hurt her.

None of that would help me find her.

Chapter 3

Aleena

My situation called for drastic measures. It happens that way sometimes. Like yesterday, the situation had called for wine and whining on the phone with Molly.

This situation called for a different sort of coping.

The ice cream kind.

I spent most of Saturday curled up on Molly's couch and slowly eating my way through a pint of ice cream. No, that was a lie. It was two pints.

It's a good thing I didn't get in this state often because I'd be as big as a house. By the time evening rolled around, my stomach ached and I was just as miserable as I had been earlier. Molly came in from work, took one look at me and shook her head.

She sat down across from me and fixed me with a determined look. "Girl, you are going to talk and you are going to talk now."

"I don't want to talk." I glared at her sullenly.

Molly leaned back and stared right back.

She still wore her work uniform.

I sighed. That uniform meant only one thing. She was serious. One thing we both had in common was as soon as we got home, we liked to change out of work clothes. It was an odd sort of way of shedding the stress of the day.

She was giving up that habitual routine in favor of girl talk.

"You might as well talk," she said. "You know I'm going to win this."

The thing was, I did know that. But I felt foolish and I felt stupid and I felt miserable and I hurt. Talking about it wouldn't help.

In fact, talking about it would make everything worse.

As though she was reading my mind, Molly leaned forward and took my hand.

"Whatever it is," she said. "Hiding from it can't help."

The knot in my throat made it hard to breathe. Molly shifted over to sit down beside me and she reached up to brush my hair back. "What is it? Did you find out he's engaged? For crying out loud, is it worse? Is he a total douchebag? He's not *married*, is he?"

"No." I looked away. My voice broke halfway through and I had to take a deep breath and wait for my voice to steady before I could say anything else. Flexing my hands in my lap, I lifted my gaze to the ceiling and willed away the tears. Then I looked at her. “I slept with him, Molly. Again. Last night.”

“Okay.” She drew the word out slowly, but she shook her head. “You’ve already done that once and we established it might not have been the best idea, but you weren’t reacting like this yesterday so what’s the problem?”

Unable to sit still, I stood up and started to pace. “I told you about that guy in high school, right?”

I wasn’t looking at her, but the dismissive sneer in her voice came through loud and clear. “That asshole? Yeah, you told me about him. Racist piece of scum. What’s that got to do with...?” Her voice trailed away.

I heard the floorboards creak under her feet as she stood up.

Arms around my middle, I stood staring out the small single window of her apartment. The view wasn’t much. It faced out over the narrow alley and into the brick of the next building, but least I wasn’t looking at her. At least she couldn’t see the expression on my face, couldn’t see how much of a fool I’d been.

“What happened?” she asked, her voice gentle but firm.

I took a deep breath. And then I told her. I didn’t go into the more intimate details. I’d promised that I would respect his privacy and I intended to keep that promise. But this wasn’t about his privacy as much as it was about his actions, and what his mother had said.

“She walked in on us. She didn’t seem

embarrassed, she didn't even seem to care about the fact that she'd walked in on her son having sex. What bothered her the most was the fact that she'd found her son having sex with the *help*." My voice cracked and I gave Molly a disgusted look. "The help! And then she told him that if he had to get something more exotic, he could have gotten it without 'bringing it home'."

For a moment, Molly said nothing. Then she exploded.

I've known plenty of redheads who don't have a temper. That's just one stereotype among many.

Molly, though, she had a temper. She ranted and raved and stomped across her apartment. She stalked by the sofa on one of her passes and grabbed a pillow, sending it hurling across the room. It hit a pretty little vase that had been on an end table by the armchair she'd somehow crammed into a corner. The vase shattered when it hit the floor. She didn't even pause.

She continued to rage and cuss and, bit-by-bit, I felt a little better. It was nice to have somebody angry on my behalf, to know that my hurt was justified.

Hey, what are girlfriends for?

I was twenty-one and I'd just now found a really good friend, but it had been worth the wait.

When she finally calmed down, she turned and looked at me. "I don't know whom I'm madder at," she said. "Him for standing there doing nothing or her for having the sheer nerve to say something like that. Did you slap her? Did you slap *him*?"

My despondency returned with a vengeance.

"No," I said. I shook my head and looked away. "I didn't know what to do. I think I said something." I scowled and then shrugged. "I told her I was from Iowa—that didn't really count as exotic. Then I got dressed and left."

It had turned into one of those surreal sort of blurs. I could remember what *she* said—all of it. But I could remember what *he* hadn't said—or done.

And I could remember that miserable, gut wrenching pain and the humiliation and the slap of shock.

If you'd never faced that kind of thing, then you *couldn't* understand it.

You also *couldn't* really explain it to someone who hadn't been there.

Being marginalized simply for not being enough of one race or another, or being poor, or being a woman, or being anything *other* is something you just don't *get* until you've faced it. I'd been facing it all my life and it wasn't any easier.

After a moment, Molly came over and wrapped an arm around my waist and just stood there, leaning against me.

She got it, I knew.

Being bisexual, even in New York, wasn't easy. I'd heard plenty of homophobic slurs thrown her way when she was out with a girl, but it was still different than it was with me. People couldn't see it when she walked down the street. Mine was painted on my skin, my eyes. Not white. Not black. Never enough to be either one.

"I don't even exist to her," I said softly. I swallowed the ache in my throat. "She talked like I wasn't even there."

"She doesn't matter." Molly hugged me tighter.

"But he does...and he just stood there."

Needing to move, I squeezed Molly back and then started to pace.

"What are you going to do?" Molly asked.

"I don't know."

"What do you *want* to do?"

"Run back to Iowa." I gave her a weak smile. "But is that really the answer?"

"I think you know it's not," she said softly. She came over and sat down on the coffee table, staring at me. Her bright hair fell into her face and she pushed it back. "You left Iowa because you weren't happy. If you go back, is that likely to change?"

"No." I dropped onto the couch and buried my face in my hands.

The *one* place I'd been happy had been here, for the past six weeks. Working for the Winter Corporation. And it hadn't *just* been because of Dominic. Yes, I loved working with him, even when he drove me crazy, but I loved my job and what I did.

"I don't know what to do, Molly."

"I think you do." She lifted a brow. "You have to face him. You have to deal with this. And you know it. Running away...Aleena, that's not you."

"And facing him is going to make me happy?" I muttered. I was grateful she didn't see me leaving Iowa to come here as running away.

Molly nibbled on her lower lip for a minute and I could tell she was thinking hard. Finally, she said, "I had a roommate for a little while not too long after I came out. I was still nervous about it. She didn't know. I mean, I wasn't telling everybody. She found out one night when she got home from work earlier than planned...I had a girlfriend with me. We were on the couch, messing around. She just kind of stared at us and then gave a little laugh like it was no big deal. After that, she started acting weird around me. It wasn't hard to figure out why. I tried to let it go and try to act like it didn't bother me, but it did. The longer I ignored it, the worse it got and the more it bothered me. And then I started noticing people treating me weird. I couldn't figure out why. Then one day Mrs. Hagerty from upstairs said something to me. I didn't know what she meant at first, but I wasn't going to let it go, so I asked her."

I just waited. She'd finish when she was ready.

Molly leaned forward, her eyes flashing. "She said that she'd heard I was doing sex shows and dirty movies on the side to make ends meet. Then she offered to help me out if I ever needed cash because I was such a sweet girl...I didn't need to do that sort of thing for money. It wasn't safe."

I gaped at her. "How did...what?"

"You heard me." She shrugged as if it didn't matter. "I'd freaked my old roommate out. She wasn't comfortable with me being bisexual so she decided to tell weird stories about me. First, it went from me having orgies up to me being a stripper and then suddenly I was having gang-bangs and selling amateur sex videos." She pushed her hair back. "The point is, I'd known all along she wasn't comfortable with me after that night she walked in on me. I should have confronted her and dealt with it, then. I didn't. But I did after that mess with Mrs. Hagerty. She tried to laugh it off like it was a joke, but then she spun me this crap about how if I slept with other women, she's pretty sure I'd have to be involved in that other dirty stuff too. And oh...*by the way,* she's not happy with me being her roommate and she has other people lined up, so how about me vacating..."

"But...this apartment, isn't it in your dad's name?"

Molly grinned. "Yes. I booted her out on her ass."

I tipped my face back to the ceiling. "What a bitch," I muttered. "Okay, so... *A- if* you were stripping for money, so what? That's your concern. And *B-* it's none of her business if you're asexual, bisexual, trisexual, metrosexual or anything else."

"Damn straight." Molly pursed her lips. "Trisexual, huh?"

I snickered. Then, drawing my legs up, I hugged them to my chest. "Dominic's not going to tell crap stories about me, Moll."

"No. But his mom might," she said.

Fuck. Squeezing my eyes shut, I pressed my

forehead to my raised knees. I hadn't even thought of that.

"Don't worry. I don't think that's likely. She sounds too image conscious. She wouldn't want the New York elite to know her precious baby slept with a girl like you." Molly's voice held enough scorn that it was clear what she thought of the word choice. "But that's not the issue, honey. You won't feel better until you confront him and deal with this. You need to find out why he just stood there and he needs to know that it hurt you."

She was right.

A hollow empty ache spread through me and I started to rock myself slowly back and forth.

After a moment, Molly came to sit beside me, curling her arm around me. She didn't say anything, but she didn't have to.

She was right. I had to go back.

***

Morning dawned cold and brittle and the sunlight had a sharp edge.

That was rather how I felt. Cold, brittle and all sharp, jagged edges.

I'd borrowed some of Molly's clothes. We weren't exactly the same size, but the nice thing about leggings was that they stretched and Molly had a couple long tunics that worked. Granted, the one I was wearing reached her knees and barely hit me mid-thigh, but I wasn't going to a club or anything. For this, it was fine.

I called for a cab. Six weeks ago, I couldn’t have afforded it, but now I could. Of course, that could change in a blink. Most likely would change. I was trying to hope for a positive outcome, but I wasn't holding my breath.

Molly came down with me and we stood chatting for the few minutes it took the cab to get there.

As it pulled to the curb, I hugged her and she kissed my cheek.

“It’ll be okay,” she said.

“How can you be so sure about that?”

“Because you’re tough and you’re going to make it okay,” she told me. “No matter how. You’ll make it okay for yourself. Call me when you need me.”

I nodded and ducked inside the cab.

She was already in her apartment building by the time the cab pulled away from the curb.

I gave him the address and leaned back, my eyes closed as he moved into the light traffic.

Most people heard a lot about New York City traffic. What people didn't hear so much about was that the traffic on the weekend wasn't all that bad. It was like half the population disappeared or went away for the weekend.

It didn’t take much time to travel from Molly’s place to central Manhattan. I opened my eyes as we drew closer to the penthouse and stared up at the bright sparkling windows of the magnificent building as it jutted up into the sky.

Sunlight bounced off the glass and I closed my eyes against the harsh glare.

"Here we are," the driver said. He recited the address to me, confirming we were at the right place.

Without responding, I used my credit card to pay for the drive.

It was odd how easily I'd adjusted to having money at my disposal. It could be gone in a blink. Soon, I'd find out whether or not I'd be going back to living on a shoestring budget.

The doorman, Stuart, saw me the moment I started walking up to the building and his eyes widened. He came rushing toward me. "Miss Aleena! Mr. Snow has been worried sick. Where have you been?"

At the sound of Dominic's name, my heart lurched. "Out." I kept my response short and sweet. Or maybe not so sweet, I decided after Stuart drew back at the abruptness of my voice.

"Are you alright?" he asked softly, almost hesitantly.

In a more moderate tone, I said, "I'm well enough. I had a rough couple of days."

I glanced upward, as though it would give me the answer to my next question. "Is he up there?"

Slowly, he shook his head. "No. Mr. Snow went to the house in the Hamptons yesterday, thinking he might find you there. He has called several times asking if you've returned. I'll call him and let him—"

"No!" I snapped, my insides freezing at the thought of seeing him. I wasn't ready.

Stuart went still. Then he looked away.

He looked terribly uncomfortable. "I'm sorry, Miss Davison, but I must let him know you're here. It was a direct order."

"An order," I said slowly. Why wasn't I surprised? I ran my tongue across my teeth and then nodded. "Fine."

Without another word, I walked inside.

***

The penthouse was quiet.

It had been cleaned and put to rights and I stood there, inside the door, staring at the couch for a moment, in the same place Jacqueline had stood on Friday. I twisted a strand of hair around my finger, imagining I could hear the murmur of his voice in my ear, the way his fingers had tangled in my hair and tugged, my skin burning under the harsh impact of his hand after he'd spanked me.

Then I went cold as I recalled his mother's words.

She might as well have backhanded me—it probably would have done less damage. Physical force was something I could have dealt with much easier. Hit her back, threaten to press charges. Ruin her precious reputation.

But the cool disdain in her eyes?

It hadn't even been hate.

I could handle hate. That had been different. Like I wasn't even worth the effort to feel anything but disapproval. I'd been dismissed, brushed aside like I didn't matter.

The sound of the phone ringing made me jump. I ignored it. I already knew who was calling. Just enough time had passed for Stuart to have spoken with Dominic and then for Dominic to have called the house phone.

When I didn't answer, I heard a faint *beep*.

His voice came rolling out.

It made me shiver.

It also made me furious.

"Aleena," he said, his voice soft. "I know you're there. Stuart called me...please answer."

"Not likely."

I shut the door behind me and calmly walked to my small apartment. Dominic continued to speak, but I deliberately blocked him out.

When I got to my apartment, I groaned. My cell phone was in there.

It was ringing now.

I walked over, picked it up and turned it off.

The phone beside the fat, comfortable armchair started to ring.

I headed into the bathroom.

I'd take a bath. There were no phones in the damn bathroom.

But halfway there, I stopped.

Dominic was probably on his way back here. I had a lock to my apartment, but I didn't trust him not to let himself in and I wanted to be left alone. He and I could fight it out later...if he cared enough.

For now, I needed time to clear my head.

I scrawled a note on a piece of paper, taped it to my door and then went back inside. Then I took a long, slow look around my apartment. Finally, my gaze landed on the fat armchair.

It would have to work.

It fit, but just barely. The apartment's entry way was small, forming an *L* shape that led into the living room. Sweating and out of breath, I stepped back and eyed the chair.

If the penthouse caught on fire while I was in the bathroom, I was screwed.

But I was willing to take that risk.

Turning on my heel, I strode into the bathroom.

Chapter 4

Dominic

The phone rang. And rang. And rang.

It took me a moment to realize that she really wasn't going to answer.

Blowing out a controlled breath, I called Stuart.

"Yes, sir?"

"She didn't leave again, did she?"

Stuart hesitated for a moment before he finally answered, "Not by this door, sir. And I have been watching almost non-stop."

I wanted to tell him that wasn't good enough, but I stopped myself. I wasn't the only one who lived in the building.

Forcing myself to count to ten, I checked the time. It would take another hour and a half to get there. There wasn't much traffic, but I couldn't make the distance any shorter. "How is she?"

"Sir?"

"Stuart, for fuck's sake." The past thirty plus hours had shattered my control. I was tired, my head hurt, I wanted some coffee and I hadn't gotten around to taking a shower before Stuart had called and told me that Aleena was there. My mood was so far down below miserable, it wasn't even funny. "How *is* she? Is she okay?"

"No." His voice was sharp.

I'd known Stuart since I'd moved into the penthouse. He was a friendly kind of guy. When he'd shown me pictures of a round, chubby-cheeked newborn baby of indeterminate sex, I'd had Fawna send a gift to him and his wife. His wife had thanked me with chocolate chip cookies and he'd thanked me with a handshake and tears in his eyes that had left me feeling uncomfortable.

And this was the first time I'd ever heard the first edge of disapproval in his voice.

I knew he adored Aleena. Just about everybody who met her did and in that short, simple answer, I'd heard a hundred things.

"She's upset, isn't she?"

"It would seem so, sir."

Flexing my hands on the steering wheel, I focused on the road. I could fix this. My mother could be a bitch and I knew it, but I had to believe it wasn't too late. "Can somebody cover for you while you go check on her?"

"It might be best, sir, if we give her some time alone."

"Dammit, Stu! She's had the whole damn weekend!"

There was another one of those faint pauses and

then Stuart, his voice stiff and formal, replied. "Of course, sir. I'll see to it."

He disconnected and I almost threw the phone out the window.

There were times when I knew I was getting close to the line into serious asshole territory. The past couple days, I suspected I'd fallen clear over. And maybe crawled a couple feet further.

***

Ninety minutes could speed by if distracted, having fun or otherwise engaged.

On the flip-side, ninety minutes could also last an eternity.

I couldn't say the ninety minutes it took to get back to Manhattan that day were the longest ninety minutes of my life. After all, I'd spent a year in hell.

But those minutes—actually, that entire weekend—had dragged by inexorably and by the time I arrived at the penthouse, I was so ramped up and ready to be *done*, I thought I'd go mad.

Okay, Aleena. We're having this out now, I thought grimly as I climbed out of the car. I rarely drove myself. I preferred to deal with business while somebody else handled the wheel, but this time around, I hadn't wanted to wait for the driver. Nor had I had the patience for speed limits. Driving had been bad enough. If I'd had to sit in the back with nothing to do but wait, I would've screamed.

Tossing my keys toward Stuart, I said, "She's still here?"

He nodded politely.

He'd called twenty minutes after we'd spoken and informed me that Aleena had requested some time alone.

Fine.

She'd had it.

We could discuss this like rational adults now.

Rational, I told myself a few minutes later as I let myself inside. A quick look around told me Aleena wasn't in the living room or the kitchen and the utter silence would have made me think she wasn't even there, but I caught a faint noise coming from her personal apartment. She was here.

Rational. Rational.... We'd be rational about it. We'd be rational and I'd be calm and I'd apologize for how my mother had acted and she'd understand and—

"Son of a *bitch*," I growled, snatching the note from the door.

She'd written me a fucking *note*?

D.

I'm tired and need time to think. Please respect this. We can talk later.

A.

"Tired?"

I wadded up the note and spun around, hurling across the wide, open steps that led down into the main area of the penthouse. She was *tired*?

Did she have any idea what I'd been going through? How scared I'd been?

I turned back and grabbed the doorknob, ready to force my way inside and demand she talk to me.

Then, slowly, I let go.

Staring at the door, I backed away.

A memory of her face as she'd looked Friday night ran through my mind and I closed my eyes.

Time.

Yeah. Okay.

I'd give her some time.

Feeling like I'd aged a decade since I'd pulled my car up to the curb, I moved slowly down the steps and sat down, her door in view.

I didn't move.

I just sat there and listened.

But other than the faint noise I could hear from her TV, I didn't hear a single thing from Aleena's apartment all night.

Chapter 5

Aleena

My alarm blared Monday morning, not that I'd needed it.

I hadn't slept more than a few hours and I'd been awake since before four. I spent the hours dealing with email and trying to prepare myself for...something.

That was the thing. I didn't know what I was preparing myself for.

We needed to talk and I knew it had to happen, but I wasn't ready to do it before we went to work.

So, we do it after.

That decision made, I was ready a good thirty minutes earlier than normal and since I knew his schedule like the back of my hand, I planned my exit strategy to coincide with the time I knew he'd be showering.

Part of me wished he'd be waiting for me.

I even held my breath as I glanced around the wide-open area that was revealed as I came down the hall that led to the stairs. But he wasn't there and I could faintly hear the low thrum of water.

Immediately, there was an image on my mind of that long, golden body standing under a fall of water and my belly got all hot and tight, my nipples hardening as they rubbed against the silk of my bra.

Before the water could shut off, I hurried down the stairs and slid out the front door.

I was down in the quiet elegance of the lobby chatting with the morning doorman when Dominic called.

"Where are you?" he demanded, his voice flat.

"Downstairs, Mr. Snow," I said calmly, although my heart skipped a few beats. "We've got a busy morning and I was going over a few things, checking on the delivery of the breakfast I ordered for the morning meeting and–"

"Fine." The word was clipped, followed by the sound of the call being cut off.

He emerged from the elevator a few minutes later and I swallowed. Convulsively, I tightened my fingers on the strap of my bag. It was a tidy little affair that served as both purse and briefcase and just then, it kept me from reaching for him.

"We need to talk," he said, coming in close and taking up all of my personal space and then some.

"I'm aware of that." I managed a cool tone. "I just don't think this is the time."

"Oh?" That single syllable seemed to carry the perfect amount of curiosity and royal demand. I had the fleeting idea that a hundred, maybe two hundred years ago, he would have been perfectly at home striding down a street in London, perhaps Paris—old world aristocracy of course—clad in a coat of velvet with one of those ruffled shirts men used to wear, over a pair of tight trousers that ended in a pair of polished boots right up to his knees, giving orders naturally and watching as the peasants scrambled to obey. We were really from different worlds.

As I looked away, Dominic reached up and brushed his thumb across my chin. "When is the time, Aleena?"

Startled by the touch—right here in public—I jerked back.

Heat...and something else...glowed in his eyes.

"I..." I cleared my throat and pretended to check the time. "Tonight, Dominic. We can talk tonight."

A muscle tensed in his jaw.

He wanted to argue with me. I could tell.

Part of me wished he would.

But that wouldn't happen. I wasn't lying. We *did* have a busy day ahead of us and Dominic had some important business meetings to attend to. That pretty much decided it right there.

For Dominic, business came first. First, last and always. Maybe if he had said, *fuck that. Fuck the meetings, we're doing this now,* it would have done something to ease the misery inside me.

But he didn't.

We left.

***

It was the day from hell, even worse than the week after the debacle with the party planner.

Everything was stilted and formal. One thing was certain. Molly hadn't been wrong when she'd said I needed to deal with this. And Dominic hadn't been wrong, either.

We had to talk.

Either I could handle what had happened Friday or not. It was as simple as that. I had to figure out if I could let it go, and if I couldn't, then I'd have to turn in my notice.

The meetings that normally fascinated me seemed boring and interminable. I pulled up reports for Dominic and jotted down notes. I made personal meetings and dealt with emails, all while on edge most of the day. Constantly, I could feel his eyes on me. When I'd look up, he would be looking elsewhere, but as soon as I looked away, I'd feel him studying me again.

It was enough to make any sane girl *crazy* and at that point, I didn't feel particularly sane.

Each minute dragged on into eternity, right up until four o'clock.

The first month leading up to the opening of Dominic's newest business, we'd often worked up until seven or later, but it had been open a few weeks now and thanks to the excellent staff he'd found, he had started leaving around five, which had left me free to do the same.

Suddenly, time didn't go slow anymore. Those seconds seemed to speed by. It was like I'd fallen through a time warp. Minutes became seconds and I would have done *anything* to slow that clock down. I still didn't know what I was going to say to him and I had no idea what he planned to say to me.

It was 4:39 when I locked myself in the bathroom. With my back to the door, I punched in a desperate message to Molly. Silencing the ring tone, I hoped and prayed she wouldn't be working.

Her response came up almost right away.

Yeah, I'm working. But I'm on my break. What's up?

I punched in my response.

We haven't talked yet. We're getting ready to after work. What am I supposed to say to him?

Her answer came up:

That's easy. Tell him what you feel. Tell him what you want.

She called that easy? Hello, I didn't even *know* what I wanted.

I told her that. She responded back in the same matter of fact, no nonsense way.

Honey, you know what you want. You want him to know that he hurt you and you want an apology and you want to know that it's not going to happen again. If that bitch of a mother of his attacks you like that again, he needs to address it. He needs to address it right then and right there and tell her she can't talk to you that way. And next time you need to be more of a bitch yourself right back to her.

I didn't know how to respond to that. She wasn't wrong.

But could I actually say that to him?

When I didn't respond right away, Molly sent me another text.

Break's wrapping up and I got to go. Look, maybe he's just into you because you're hot and sexy and he wants you. If that's the case, find out, deal with it and move on because you deserve more. But if it could be more...if it is more, you've got to talk to him and work it out. You've got a right to expect him to care about you and he should know he hurt you. Either you two have something or you don't. If you do, you've got a right to know these things. And if he cares about you, you've got a right to expect these things. And you owe it to yourself to stand up for yourself. You deserve better.

Two seconds later, another message came through.

Love you sweetie. Stand up. You can do it.

Pressing my head against the door, I clutched the phone tightly. Stand up.

Five o'clock rolled around and I gathered my things. But Dominic wasn't in the office.

After a few moments, I went out to where his administrative assistant worked. The two of us had gotten to know each other fairly well and she shot me a look that managed to bring a weary smile to my face.

"I don't know about you, but that was one lousy Monday," Amber said softly as she held out a note. "From Mr. Snow."

"Yeah." I nodded in agreement and then looked down at the note.

I managed not to make any reaction as I read it and gave her a faint smile when I looked back up. "I'll see you in the morning."

The note, I crumpled in my hand.

You can take the car home. I'll be there later this evening.

So much for talking.

And I supposed that answered the unspoken question about what I meant to him.

I had Chinese delivered. Listlessly poking at the beef and broccoli for a few minutes, I gave up and just finished off the hot and sour soup, staring out my window into the park. I wanted summer. I wanted longer days so I could take walks in the evening. I also wanted warmth and sunlight and something other than the chill in the air when I went outside.

I was stirring the dregs of the soup when the penthouse door opened.

I waited.

But he didn't come in.

Leaning back, I stared up at the ceiling. I could hear him moving around in his room and I shoved back, gathering up my trash.

He was going to jerk me around like a puppet on a string? Fine. If he wanted to talk, he could come find me when he was ready.

Controlling bastard.

I settled in my room and started to flip through the channels. I rarely watched TV anymore. Barely read. Didn't do anything that didn't involve work. I wondered if maybe—

My door opened.

Slowly, I turned my head and found Dominic filling the entrance.

He flicked a look around my room and then his gaze came to me. "Perhaps now is a good time to have that talk."

Slowly, I rose. Thumbing off the TV, I put the remote down and moved over to the window. The view faced out over Manhattan and the lights and spires of the buildings turned the skyline into a jewel-bedecked panorama.

"Talk," I said. I glanced at him over my shoulder and realized I was smiling. It was a humorless, bitter sort of smile.

Stand up, Molly had told me. Yeah. I think maybe I needed to do that.

"Sure, Dominic. We can talk."

Dominic's gaze slid down to my mouth, then away.

I guess the smile wasn't a pleasant one because he didn't smile back. That was fine. I hadn't meant it to be nice. I went back to gazing out over the city.

I had to know where I stood. Where *we* stood and I had to know soon.

This was just too hard. Either we had something or we didn't, but if we did...

"I'm sorry about what my mother said, how she acted," Dominic said quietly, his voice oddly formal, almost strained.

Leaning my head against the pane of glass, I whispered softly, "You're sorry...for your mother."

The silence that followed was awful.

When he finally spoke, it was in that same stiff, formal voice and the sound of it made me flinch. "I realize, looking back, that I should have said something. I didn't. I'm sorry for that."

"Are you?" I asked quietly.

When he didn't say anything, I turned and looked at him.

He had turned away. His back was rigid, his shoulders a hard, solid line. He looked so unapproachable.

That was fine. Just then, I didn't think I could have handled the idea of approaching him anyway.

I think it's time to figure out just where I stand. The longer I stared at him, the more I realized I needed to know. "Do we have anything here?"

It was a simple enough question, I thought. I didn't know a whole lot about guys, but I did know that guys didn't like to talk about emotions and the general idea of relationships could make a guy gun shy. But the decent ones would man up and deal, right? Especially after something like what had happened.

I'd thought Dominic was one of the decent ones. I was starting to believe I'd been wrong.

He turned and looked at me, his gaze remote. “Of course we do. I think we've covered everything we need to cover, Aleena. I am sorry for what happened Friday. I assure you it won't happen again.”

He was almost to the door when I spoke. I couldn't see him through the tears in my eyes and I silently cursed myself for not being able to do this without sounding like a simpering ex.

“Damn right it won't.” I blinked away the tears and managed to at least keep my voice steady. “I quit, Mr. Snow. I'll work out the time needed for you to find a new assistant, but this arrangement clearly isn't working.”

I started for my bedroom. I needed to get as far away from him as I could. Antarctica sounded ideal.

Before I could open the door, one hand closed around the doorknob. He grabbed my arm with the other hand and spun me around.

“What?” he demanded. There was more emotion in his face than I'd seen all evening. No, this was the most emotion I'd seen in him since that monstrous woman he called his mother had walked in on us.

“You heard me. This isn't working for me.” Jutting my chin up, I repeated what I'd said only moments ago. “I *quit*.”

Dominic's mouth came down on mine.

I locked my jaw when his tongue stroked across

my lips, demanding entrance. Despite the heat that twined and stroked through me, I refused to give in. After a few moments, he lifted his head.

"Why?" He remained tantalizingly close. Tormenting close. It was enough to drive me out of my mind.

"Are you *serious*?" I shoved him away. I had both regret and relief when he went.

Stepping aside, I darted past him and strode out of my apartment, toward the stairs. I'd just leave if I had to. If he touched me again, I'd probably give in, and I couldn't do that.

"I already told you I was sorry!" he shouted.

I stopped at the top of the stairs and turned around to face him. My temper was rising and I was tired of keeping it down. "And then when I asked if we had anything going on, you stiffened up like I'd shoved a hot poker up your ass!"

His reaction to that was...off.

He went white. So pale, like all of the blood had been drained. He turned away so I couldn't see his face. Bracing his hands against the wall, he stared down. "What is it you want, Aleena? Help me out here."

"Is it really that complicated?" My hands were shaking and I couldn't tell if it was only anger or if desire was mixed in there. "I can't do this back and forth thing, okay? I need to know where I stand with you. Do we have anything going on between us? Do you *care* about me? Because *I* don't know. I've never done this before."

His answer was so quiet, I wasn't entirely sure I'd heard him right.

"Neither have I."

"What?" Confusion took the edge off my anger.

He lifted his head and stared at me, eyes glittering. "Neither have I."

"But..." I flicked a hand, waving the idea off. I didn't want to stop being angry. I needed it to keep from being hurt again. "Dominic, you've been around the block more times than a marathon runner."

"No." His lip curled, an almost ironic, dismissive sort of sneer. "I've had sex. I've had sexual relationships and I've had lovers and I've escorted women to and from social events. None of them have ever gone as far as to ask me if I *cared* about them. And they wouldn't have bothered because they knew the answer would be *no*."

Something cold went through me, extinguishing the anger and leaving...nothing. My gaze fell away from his and I started to back up. I'd wanted an answer and I'd gotten one.

Before I could get to the steps, he was there. His hands came up and caught my arms. "But you aren't..." An unfamiliar look drifted across his face. He looked hesitant, uncertain even.

Dominic Snow never looked uncertain.

"I don't do relationships, Aleena. It's an ironic twist that I decided to play around with a matchmaking company. Love is all well and good for others, but I don't believe in it for myself." Then he lifted a hand and pushed it into my hair. “I’ve never even wanted to care about a woman...until you came along.”

The look he gave me left me feeling stripped bare and if it wasn’t for the massive pain I felt inside, I might have...well, I don’t know what I might have done. Because that agonizing emptiness inside was about to devour me. It was about ready to just eat me alive and I couldn’t think past it.

“You care,” I said, my voice hitching. Dammit. “Or you think you care.”

“Aleena...”

I tugged his hand away and stepped to the side to put some distance between us. “Why are you apologizing to me, Dominic?”

He stood there, staring at me, confusion on his face. Finally, he shoved a hand through his hair. It tumbled right back into place. The unkempt hair and the tight set of his jaw gave him a slightly edgy look, a slightly wild look, a slightly wicked look. I curled my fingers into fists and rested them behind me. I wanted to reach for him. So bad.

“I already told you. Look...” He stopped and sighed. “My mother has this class issue. I hate it, but I can’t *change* her. I should have said something and I didn’t. I’m sorry.”

“Oh...your mother has a lot more problems than issues with class,” I said and this time, I didn’t hold back the scorn, or the anger I felt. It burned away some of the pain, or at least hid it.

Dominic’s eyes narrowed slightly. “Aleena, half

the people I know—no, more than that—tend to have class issues. I don't like it, but it's not like I'm friends with them. I don't hang out with them. I'm not looking for friendship or anything with them. It's just how they are."

"How they are." I nodded. "And let me explain just *how* they are. If they're anything like your mother, they're racist, narrow-minded elitist assholes."

Dominic jerked his head back as if I'd slapped him. "She's not—"

I took a step forward, letting the little spark inside me burst into a full-fledged flame. "Don't you *dare* tell me she's not racist! What the hell? You think she was calling me *exotic* because I'm not *rich*?"

"Aleena..." He opened his mouth, closed it. I could see in his eyes that he knew.

"You've never been in my shoes. You can't know what it's like." I curled my hands into fists so he couldn't see them shaking. "Now I'm pretty sure if I was some little blond-haired, blue-eyed white girl and she walked in on us, she might have been plenty disgusted, but it goes a lot deeper than that. Because I'm *not*. She saw me, saw a *little colored girl*...she saw your *hired help* and she totally dismissed me as a person. I'm *not* a person to her."

Tears burned my eyes now and I swiped them away as they fell. "And you just sat there."

He reached for me.

I held up a hand. "Don't. I can't—" My voice

broke and I just shook my head.

The silence that fell was horrible. My heart felt like it was going to split in two as I struggled to get the tears under control. I didn't want to break in front of him. I *wouldn't* break in front of him. After a few moments, I managed to stop the flood and I stared at him. He looked...lost.

"Why did you just sit there?" I asked. "I told you about what had happened to me before. You *knew* how much her words would hurt me and you just sat there."

Dominic looked around and finally, he just slid down to the floor. It was...incongruous. I did the same thing, taking up the space on the wall opposite him, and staring at his pale face.

"I'm adopted," he said softly.

Those were the last two words I expected him to start this conversation off with. I said nothing, just stared and waited for him to make sense.

"I..." He drove his head back against the wall, hard. Hard enough to hurt, I'd think, but he didn't even blink. "My mother and I haven't had a good—or easy—relationship in...well. Ever. I know she loves me, but things were never easy. I think she thought she'd be getting this sweet, quiet, gentle little doll she could dress up in doll clothes and parade around in front of her friends and then she could put me back in a box until it was time for the next occasion to show me off."

The words weren't bitter, just matter-of-fact.

"I don't know who my birth mother is. For all I

know, she was...” He sneered now, infusing the words with the patrician tones I didn't doubt he'd heard from his mother. “Some *‘low-class tramp of a girl’*.” He angled his head to the side. “That wasn't the first time she’d walked in on me with a woman, Aleena. And that phrase? That was what she said to a girl I’d brought home with me when I was a teenager. She was a nice girl. I...I think I could have liked her. But she ran out crying after that and never talked to me again.”

“It sounds like your mother enjoys belittling people,” I said.

“She does.” Dominic’s mouth tightened. “I love her, but I don’t really like her.”

With a start, I realized that I felt sorry for him. Sorry for this rich, privileged man who'd grown up with the proverbial silver spoon in his mouth. Folding my hands in my lap, I thought back over my childhood and realized that maybe it hadn’t been as rough as I’d thought. Yeah, I’d often been ostracized—I'd been the outsider, but some had been through choice. I’d been smart and not like the flirty, giggly girls who cared about clothes and gossip. And I'd been the girl who was never quite white enough or never quite black enough to be accepted into either social circle.

But I had parents who loved me and worked hard to make a good life for me. No matter how bad things had gotten at school, I'd always known that I had a refuge at home.

“She didn’t know how to handle me and my

dad…" Dominic shrugged. "He just ignored me. Neither of them knew what to do with a kid, so I…well. I sort of ran wild. I ran *really* wild. It took…some things to happen for me to get my act together and there are still a lot of issues between me and my mom. I don't even talk to my dad, so she's all I have. But when she starts talking about class…"

"You think of your birth mother," I said, understanding dawning.

His eyes came to mine.

"Does she know anything about your birth mother?"

"I've never outright asked." Dominic jerked a shoulder in a shrug. "I…" He abruptly shot to his feet, the motion so sudden, it caught me off guard. "When I say there are problems between my mother and I, I mean *serious problems*. She uses guilt like a personal accessory and half the time, I just maintain the status quo. It's easier. I never…"

It was my turn to come to my feet and he turned to me.

"When you've never been on the receiving end, Dominic, it's probably pretty easy to overlook something like racism—especially the casual kind." I crossed my arms over my chest. "It's not like she stood there and shrieked at you about daring to sleep with a black girl. Subtle racism though…it's just as real. It's just as ugly."

"It won't happen again," he said, his voice rough and tight.

I shook my head. “It will. You already said, you can’t change how she thinks and you know you can’t change how she acts. But the next time she does it...I won’t just *sit* there. And—”

He cut me off, his hands cupping my face while one thumb pressed to my mouth.

“I won’t just sit there either,” he promised. “I won't let her do that again.”

Chapter 6

Aleena

Still staring at him, I held my breath until his thumb slid over my lower lip, then fell away.

I licked my lips, tasting him there.

His gaze dropped to my mouth. But he took a step back.

Without even thinking, I moved closer.

"I..." I took a deep breath. "Okay, so you said you haven't done relationships. If that's what this is, what it's going to be, I think we just had what probably counts as our first fight, followed by our first make-up." My stomach twisted, but I forced myself to go forward. Dominic may have been the dominant one when it came to sex, but it was clear, he was going to need a push here. "Now this is where—and I could be wrong—but I think this is where we are supposed to have make-up sex."

Dominic's eyes darkened. "Is that a fact?" His voice was low, rough.

I nodded, my face heating as he watched me.

“Just what is make-up sex? What does it entail?”

I shrugged. “I think that’s up to us and what we want. You’ve pretty much made it clear you’re not the hearts and flowers sort of guy, so...”

He reached towards me, wrapping his large hands around my wrists.

“No. I don’t do hearts and flowers,” he said.

He backed me up against the wall and dragged my hands up, held them there. Then he leaned in and kissed me, a hot, open-mouthed kiss that left me sighing in dazed hunger when he finally shifted his attention to my jaw.

“I could give you hearts and flowers though,” he said into my ear. “Is that what you want?”

“I just want you.” The confession was barely a whisper.

For a brief moment, he didn't move and I wondered if he'd heard me.

Then he leaned back and stared at me. “Leave your hands up,” he said.

I did, although they slid down some without the support from his.

He cocked a brow, but said nothing, reaching for the big, fuzzy buttons that held my sweater closed. I’d changed after I came home, needing something familiar to comfort me. My favorite sweater and leggings had seemed to fit the bill.

He opened the sweater, but didn’t remove it. It hung open down my torso as he freed the front catch on my bra. “I think I like this style of bra on you,” he said as he slid one hand up to cup my breast, pausing to pluck at my nipple.

I gasped when he gave a particularly hard tug that sent jolts of heat arrowing down to my pussy. How did he know exactly what I needed?

He continued on his path after that, shoving his hands into my leggings and panties, shoving them down, but not completely stripping them away. When I was half naked, he backed away and just stared at me.

I felt terribly exposed, somehow more naked than if he had stripped me completely.

He slid a hand down the midline of my body, from my sternum to my navel and on down until he could slide the tip of his fingers through the thin curls gathered between my thighs. I whimpered and shoved myself forward, seeking out his touch.

He immediately stopped.

"I didn't tell you that you could move." There was no doubting that tone.

Anticipation flooded me and he tugged me off the wall.

"Kneel, Aleena."

I went to my knees, uncertain what to do with my hands, but I figured it out a moment later.

He used the flat of his hand between my shoulder blades and nudged me forward until I was on my hands and knees, then kept on pushing until my face was on the ground, my ass up in the air.

I didn't even have time to brace myself before he spanked me.

It was hard and almost too painful, but heat still exploded through me. I cried out, squeezing my eyes closed.

He did it again and again and then I felt him plunging two fingers inside me.

I came, hard and fast.

I didn't even have a chance to come down from it before he drove inside me. The slick, cool feel of his cock told me he'd donned a condom at some point. He thrust deep, deep, deep...forcing me to stretch to accommodate him.

When he could go no farther, he stopped.

Then he spanked me again.

Another thrust.

Then he slapped my other cheek.

He kept that rhythm up until I was sobbing and begging for release. And then he stopped and stroked the pads of his fingers against the sensitive skin of my bottom. I quivered, tensed in anticipation, but all he did was wait for me to calm.

It took *forever*.

Denied the pleasure of orgasm, I was about ready to sob when he started to fuck me again.

He did it over and over, taking me to the edge and then stopping right when I was ready to come.

My leggings were trapped around my knees, my sweater and bra still caught and tangled around my arms and shoulders. My body was shaking so badly that I couldn't have moved even if I'd been free.

I gasped when he tangled a hand in my hair and forced my head up, bending my back to an almost unnatural degree. I could feel the muscles cramping.

Now he moved slower inside me, his cock swelling and rasping against my walls. He caught my hand and guided it between my thighs. “Touch yourself.”

I tried to pull my hand away. I didn't want to make myself come. I wanted him to do it.

“Do it, Aleena...or I’ll pull out and you won’t come tonight. Not from me.”

“Bastard,” I snarled, a sudden flare of anger going through me. Then I tensed, remembering that I'd been punished simply for speaking out of turn. Had I gone too far?

To my surprise, he laughed and drove hard and high up into me, eliciting a high-pitched sound I'd never made before.

“Do it.”

I did, still angry, but needing release more.

And finally, he let me come.

After, he carried me to bed. His bed. He slid me under the covers and then stretched out behind me, not touching but close enough for me to feel the heat from his body.

“I think for our first round of make-up sex, that went pretty well,” Dominic said. He sounded casual, but there was a world of uncertainty lying under it.

“I'm pretty sure the person who's in the wrong is the one who's supposed to be punished.” Despite the pleasure throbbing through my body, I couldn't quite hide the anger in my voice.

The bed shifted as he moved and suddenly he

was above me. “You're angry with me.”

Now that we were done, I could feel all of the pushed down emotions starting to come up. “You were the one who screwed up, but I'm on my hands and knees getting beaten like some kid who got caught doing something wrong.” Tears burned in my eyes.

“Why didn't you say your safe word?” There was a tinge of annoyance in his question.

I sat up, wincing as my ass rubbed against the sheets. I held the sheet against my breasts even though it was dark in the room and he'd already seen me naked. “I'm sorry if I'm not *experienced* enough in this to automatically think of that when my ass is burning.” I spit the words out and started to climb off the bed.

“Aleena.” He put his hand on my arm.

I almost shook it off. I hadn't told him to stop. He hadn't forced me. I just hadn't realized...I forced myself to say it. “The first night we were together...I knew that wasn't how you liked sex. And then the other night...I enjoyed it. I'd just thought...” The tears spilled over and I wiped at them, hating myself for crying, but unable to stop it.

“Thought what?” His voice was soft and closer than before. He was right behind me. “Talk to me, please.”

“Nothing.”

“Aleena.”

It was that commanding tone that hit something deep inside me. “You hurt me, Dominic.” He caught his breath and I quickly clarified what I meant. "I don't mean physically. I mean, my ass hurts, but that's not the point. What you did, or didn't do, with your mom, it hurt me, and then you say you're sorry."

"I am."

"But then, instead of..." My voice hitched. "Instead of taking care of me and showing me how sorry you were, you treated me like...like I was just there to be used."

"Used you." There was pain in those words. His arms went around me, pulling me back to him, pulling me onto his lap. "Oh, baby, I'm so sorry." He kissed my forehead. "I didn't think."

I wanted to push him away and leave. To quit like I'd originally said I would. I also wanted to press myself closer to his chest and never leave.

"I promised to teach you and then I fucked it up." His hand moved up and down my arm slowly. "I let myself get caught up in how much I wanted you and forgot how innocent you are."

I almost laughed at that, but I let him talk. I needed to know what he was thinking before I could decide what I wanted to do.

"A good Dominant is supposed to take care of the Submissive in the relationship, but sex was never about a relationship or emotions. There were clear rules set in place before sex, and I never had to worry about...after. I'm good at dominating in the bedroom, at making sure my partner comes, but this...this is a part of it that's new to me." He took my chin between his thumb and forefinger, tilting my head so our eyes met. “I failed to do my part.” He brushed his fingers across my cheek. “All I thought about was wanting to make you come, and I didn't even consider how it would...” He looked away.

“Hey.” I reached up and put my hand on his cheek, turning his face back to me. “It's okay. I understand.” And I did. He'd thought he was making it up to me by making me come so hard I couldn't see straight. On that part, he'd succeeded.

“It's not okay.” His expression was serious. “I don't know if I can *not* be this way, not be in control.”

“I'm not asking you to be submissive.” I didn't fully understand what the capital 'S' term meant, but I knew enough to get my point across. “But I need you to teach me what it means to be in your world.” I swallowed hard. “But only if you want this to be more than sex. I can't do this if this is all there is.”

He captured my hand and turned his head, kissing my palm. “What did I ever do to deserve you?” he murmured. He turned back towards me. “I want more.”

My heart gave a wild leap. He bent his head and brushed his lips across mine, a gentle touch.

“Now, lay down on your stomach.”

I stared at him. He couldn't be serious.

“Part of being a Sub means obeying when your Dom tells you something,” he said. “Trusting him.” He tucked my hair behind my ear. “And that means the Dom has to earn the trust.” He kissed my temple. “Please, Aleena.”

I did as he said, my stomach clenching. I heard him moving around, but couldn't see well enough to see what he was doing. Suddenly, the scent of cinnamon filled the air. He moved the sheet and I sucked in a breath when I felt his hands on my ass. As he began to rub what I assumed was lotion into my stinging skin, I started to relax, the pain fading.

He paused for a moment and leaned down to kiss my shoulder blade. “We can do this.”

I didn't say anything as he went back to massaging in the soothing lotion. He was right. We were in new territory for both of us, but we could do it.

Chapter 7

Aleena

"I can't, Mom."

I kept my attention focused on the planner in front of me. I had my tablet flat on the table and both my phone and Dominic's beneath it as I added a series of meetings, parties, lunches, breakfasts, brunches—Friday was going to be hell. We had breakfast, brunch, lunch *and* a tea scheduled.

Tea.

What in the world was I supposed to wear for *tea*?

He was meeting somebody who was flying in from England and I'd been told to set up tea.

So I'd talked with Amber. While I handled his personal day-to-day schedule, my job was a cakewalk compared to hers. She dealt with the ins and outs of the Winter Corporation and moved from one business to another, depending on which arm needed her the most. Right now, it was *Trouver*

L'Amour and we'd ended up talking to Fawna. Between the three of us—or rather between Amber and Fawna, with me making notes and listening intently, tea was now on the schedule. I rarely had a chance to eat much at these meetings, so I wasn't worried about eating myself sick.

No, the real problem was going to be staying on top of everything.

The meetings were all business related, but that didn't keep Dominic from keeping both me and Amber with him. It was mentally exhausting and I understood why Fawna had always kept such thorough notes.

I'd never realized anybody could have a life as complicated as Dominic.

I was constantly recording details, looking up information and having to dig up information from the previous week.

It was a good thing I was organized and detail-oriented because Dominic was not.

Unless...

A hand landed on my thigh.

I caught my breath.

He was staring at me.

"I'm afraid I can't do lunch on Friday."

Swallowing, I leaned forward and grabbed his phone, bringing up the already crammed schedule and showing it to him. Dominic barely glanced at it. "I'm booked from about seven right up until I plan on dropping down on my couch in the evening with a beer in my hand, Mom." His fingers traced a path on my inner thigh and my nipples tightened.

I wanted to lean into his touch, but at the same time, I wanted to put some distance between us.

His eyes closed and he blew out a breath, but he didn't stop touching me either. "I'll have to have Aleena see when my schedule clears up some." Then he arched a brow and gave me a twisted sort of smile. "Would you like her number, Mom?"

Even I heard the sharp sound of her *No* as it cracked through the phone. I frowned.

His fingers tightened on my thigh for a moment. "Right, then. I'll get back to you when I have a better idea when I'll have some free time."

He hung up the desk phone without looking, his free hand back to tracing a pattern on my thigh.

"You realize..." I had to pause and steady my voice before I could continue. It was insanely difficult to concentrate with the nerves in my leg shooting electricity straight up to my groin. "You realize I have absolutely no desire to talk to her, right?"

"Oh, I know that." Dominic's blue eyes glowed with banked need. "And I knew she wouldn't accept. It got her off the phone, though, didn't it?"

He pulled his hand away and said, "We've worked enough." He checked the time and went to stand up.

"We need to finish making sure all the schedules are down for the next few weeks." I shook my head even though my body was screaming at me to beg him to touch me again. "You have some meetings in your calendar that aren't in mine. If you'd let me sync them..."

"No." His gaze slid back to the hem of my skirt and I squirmed uncomfortably. He might as well have been looking at me in my underwear, the way he watched me. But after a moment, he sighed and looked back at the agenda. "Okay, let's finish—or at least find a stopping point. Oh, leave some time open the first week in April."

"April?" I waited for more information, but he just made a low noise of affirmation in his throat.

Sighing, I continued to go through the calendars, checking things off and asking a few questions. Sometimes, it took him a couple of minutes to think back. The man was so sharp, it astounded me sometimes, but I'd come to realize his brain was like a giant metal filing cabinet. All the information was there, but he had to flip through the folders to find it because he was already on to something else.

Restless, I raised from my chair, stretching my legs as I leaned forward, one hand braced as I finished flipping through the tablet. The calendar on it was the main one. Dominic might not let me sync his to mine, but once I had everything from his agenda transferred to this one, I'd just sync this one to mine and be done with it.

Everything matched up—

I gasped as Dominic slid his hand up my leg, under my skirt.

"Dominic, we're in the—"

"Sir."

I swallowed. We'd spent some time discussing the role he'd be teaching me. Once I'd been sure he understood I would only be submissive when it came to sex, I'd been fine with it. I just hadn't realized that sex would be taking place outside of the house or a hotel room.

"Say it, Aleena."

"Sir..." It came out in a slow, shaky breath and heat exploded through me as he cupped my ass. "Sir, we're in the office."

"I know. I locked the door earlier."

Instinctively, I glanced at the door and then I found myself staring at the windows. The nearest building wasn't that far away. "The windows."

"Nobody can see in. Privacy treatment." His finger brushed against the soft cotton of my panties. "I want to fuck you here, Aleena. If you don't want me to take you standing up, bend over my desk." He paused and then asked, "You remember the word?"

"Yes, sir."

"Bend over."

I did. I felt his hands on my skirt, but he didn't pull it down. He pushed it up, baring my simple black panties. I wished I'd worn something sexier, but I hadn't been thinking I'd be doing this at work today.

"I've been watching you in this skirt all day and thinking about doing just this," he said. "Pushing it up and staring at you, open for me, then sliding my dick inside you. Would you like me to do that?"

I nodded then gasped as he brought his hand down on my ass. "Yes, sir!"

"Keep your voice down," he warned.

I sensed more than heard him standing up and then he bent over me, his hands on either side of my shoulders, his body covering me.

"I want to hear you tell me what you want, Aleena. Be a good little Sub and do that for me."

Heat flooded my face and I darted a glance at him. "I..." Swallowing, I hesitantly said, "I want you to..."

"Slide my dick in you," he prompted. "Tell me you want to feel my cock inside you."

He'd barely touched me and I was already wet and aching for him, just from that. "I want to feel your cock inside me...sir."

"Good girl."

He pulled down my panties, carefully helping me step out of them, and then placed them on the table—*arranged* them, like he was placing them on display. "I'm going to put them in my pocket when we're done," he told me. "You're going to walk out of here with nothing under your skirt. Am I understood?"

I nodded.

His theatrical sigh left my skin prickling in anticipation and he slapped me, hard and fast, three times on my ass. "I think you like being punished, Aleena."

"Yes, sir." And it was true. When we were like this, I understood that while he was in control, I did have my own power. Obedience. My safe word.

His soft laugh drew my nipples tight.

"Don't move."

I didn't dare. I wasn't even sure if I could.

I heard the foil rip and knew he was getting a condom ready. As much as I hated having anything between us, I knew there was no swaying him and now, I didn't care. If he was putting a rubber on, that meant he'd be inside me soon.

I felt the head of his cock probing me and I whimpered.

He stopped.

He didn't just *stop*, either.

He pulled out entirely and turned me to face him.

Shaking with need and nerves, I stared at him. I didn't understand.

"You have to be quiet." He smoothed my hair back from my face as he looked at me. "Can you be quiet, Aleena?"

Now I got it. Ducking my head, I whispered, "I don't know, sir."

It was becoming instinctive now, calling him *sir* when we were like this. I clamped my knees together when he stroked his thumb over my lip. "I'll help you," he said after a moment, his voice firm, as if he'd made a decision.

"Help..." And then I watched numbly as he reached up and started to loosen his tie.

He caught sight of my expression. I don't know if I looked terrified or excited. It was a mixture of both. He continued what he was doing and stopped when the tie hung loose around his neck. He cupped my face and leaned in, the touch of his mouth surprisingly gentle considering the tension I could feel radiating off of him.

"I..." Licking my lips, I whispered against his mouth. "If you use that, how can...um...I can't say...um...the word if you have me gagged?"

"Does the idea of being gagged scare you?" There was genuine concern in his voice and I knew he was remembering what had happened last night.

"A little." *A lot.*

"And does it turn you on?"

"A little." *A lot.*

That smile—that arrogant, pleased smile that I was coming to love—curled his lips. He kissed me again, just a brief one but a bit harder. "Then trust me."

He reached behind me and a moment later, he was pushing my panties in my hands. "You're going to hold onto these. If you want me to stop at any time, you just drop them. I'll see it and I'll stop. Okay?"

Nervous, I clamped the damp cotton in my hands and nodded. "Okay."

"Yes, sir," he reminded me, pressing his thumb to my lip.

"Yes, sir."

It was the last thing I would say for some time.

He used the tie as a gag. My heart was already racing and heat flooded my face as my phone chirped. "You're not available," Dominic said, no emotion in his voice. A moment later, the desk phone rang and he repeated himself as he finished adjusting the tie.

It cut ever so slightly into the corners of my mouth. "Is that comfortable?"

I shrugged and his eyes darkened for a moment.

"I can't know if it hurts if you're not honest. Don't tell me what you think I want to hear." He slid his finger under the edge of the tie at the side of my mouth and frowned. The gag loosened ever so slightly and he ran his fingers over my cheek. "I'm not a sadist. I don't want you in pain. I want to control your pleasure."

Well, damn, if that didn't just make me even more wet.

"Now, are you going to be honest with me?"

I nodded and that smile flashed again.

The desk phone rang again as I stood there, skirt up over my ass, my panties in my hands while Dominic's tie served as a gag. It didn't feel real.

Dominic watched me intently as he reached out, but he didn't answer the phone. He pushed the intercom button and when Amber answered, he said, "We're in the middle of something complicated here and we're going to be tied up for a little while. Take messages for all calls." He paused, grinned at me and then added, "Actually, just turn off the phone for the day."

There was a faint pause and both of us heard the surprise and then pleasure in her response. "Yes, sir,

Mr. Snow."

When he let go, he focused all the intensity of those blue eyes on me.

"Now..." he murmured, bending down to whisper in my ear. "Where were we?"

I took a deep breath in through my nose to brace myself. Or at least that was my intent.

He spun me around and bent me over, my hands automatically going out to brace myself. It took only seconds and before my head stopped wheeling around, he was already balls-deep inside me.

I screamed into the gag.

He pulled out and drove in again with near-bruising force. I arched up, my body straining to take him, whimpering low in my throat.

He fucked me hard and rough and fast and I screamed and moaned and mentally cursed the gag that kept me from begging him for more.

***

The next day, I worked at home alone.

Dominic had a day full of international business meetings and he'd been up well before dawn, out the door by six.

My body was still singing with the aches from our...ah...desk play yesterday, but I felt more than a little wistful as I stood staring into the empty kitchen.

No notes.

No messages on the machine.

He was focused on business and I wasn't on his mind at all.

After a breakfast of toast and tea, I sat down to get to work and ended up not stopping until I heard a perfunctory knock on the door and realized it was time for Francisco to make one of his regular appearances.

I caught sight of him, juggling bags and two gallons of milk.

Rushing over to help, I smiled at him. “Heya, ‘Cisco.”

“Aleena.” He beamed at me. Unlike most of the staff Dominic hired, he was just a few years older than me and didn’t insist on tagging *Miss* onto my name.

“You got anything yummy planned for us this week?”

“Don’t I always?”

Ready for a distraction, I helped him unpack the food he’d brought and answered the door when one of the doormen from downstairs hauled in the rest of his purchases. Francisco didn’t just prepare the meals for Dominic. He also did the weekly shopping, insisting that he’d prepare better meals if we had quality ingredients on hand.

I had to admit, I tended to cook more if there was fresh produce and meats lying around. I hated to see anything go to waste.

“How’s the saxophone player you’re seeing?” I

asked him as I pulled out bags of tomatoes and red bell peppers, celery and carrots.

He wagged his eyebrows at me. "She is...amazing, Aleena. Amazing. I think she's an angel who fell from the skies."

"Please tell me you didn't use that line on her."

"Of course not." He puffed out his thin chest. "I wanted her to say *Yes, Cisco. I'll go out to dinner with you, Cisco.* And eventually, *I'll marry you, Cisco.* Cheesy lines like that won't get me *anywhere*, bella."

I grinned at him.

"You're going to let me teach you how to cook today?"

I eyed my work. I'd already done a lot and I probably wouldn't be able to work when he was here anyway. He liked to sing to himself when he cooked, and staying on key was not one of his talents. "Sure. Let's cook."

***

"So..."

I lay in the tub, staring up at the ceiling and listening to Molly on the Bluetooth. "So...everything seems fine."

"Anything else happen with the monster mom?"

I reached for my wine and made a face she couldn't see. "No."

I didn't want to talk about me. I wanted a distraction. I couldn't see outside, but I could read a clock. Dominic should've been home hours ago.

"But you two are okay?"

"I...I think so. The guy doesn't understand relationships, Moll. I've never in been one, but I think he just doesn't...get them. And there's some messed up shit between him and his mom. I told him how I felt about everything and it was like I'd hit him across the head." I frowned, thinking about some of the reactions he'd had and then shaking my head. "I'll tell you one thing—if he had anybody decent around him when he was growing up, it was probably a miracle."

"He gets it, though, right? That he hurt you?"

"Yeah. He—" I went quiet at the sound of my name. "Hold on, Moll."

I muted the conversation and called out. "I'm...um...I'm upstairs. Hold on..."

I unmuted. "I think I need to go. I'm in the tub and he's calling for me. Probably some work that came up."

She snorted. "Yeah, I bet it's *work* that came up." She disconnected while I half-choked on a protest I didn't really believe.

I went to stand up and the door opened.

Immediately, I sank back down in the water, my face flushed.

Dominic stood there, a small smile on his lips.

"Um...I..."

He held a plate of pasta in his hands and, eyes

on me, leaned his shoulder against the door, making it clear he wasn't going anywhere. "I'm interrupting. Please continue."

"Ah..."

He swirled some linguine around a fork and I watched as he slid it between his lips. No one should be able to make eating pasta look that sexy. "Don't let me stop you."

"I'm just taking a bath," I said lamely. Water lapped at my breasts. A moment ago, my nipples had been soft from the water, but now they were tight and the motion of the water felt like a caress.

"Then take it. I was going to ask you to go over a few things while I ate, but..." His gaze slid lower.

When his eyes returned to my face, we were both breathing harder. "Do you want me to leave?" he asked softly.

I opened my mouth, about ready to tell him yes. What came out shocked the hell out of me.

"The first time I took a bath in here, I lay in this tub, touching myself and thinking about you."

His eyes flashed. Hot and bright. Harsh flags of color rode his cheeks, but his voice was calm as he said, "Is that a fact, Ms. Davison?"

"Yes, sir."

He casually took another bite of his pasta and came into the bathroom, looking as comfortable and at ease as he would in the boardroom of the Winter Corporation.

"Tell me," he said, leaning back against the deep green marble that made up the sink. "Just how did you go about this?"

I bit my lip and then slid my hand down my belly.

"I asked for you to tell me, not give me a demonstration."

I had to pause and take a deep breath before I could say anything. "I touched myself...sir."

"So you've said. But how did you do it?"

"With my fingers. Inside my..." I licked my lips. I'd never said anything like this before. "Inside my pussy. And I touched my clitoris."

He nodded. "Very good. Do you like to touch yourself?"

"Sometimes." I shrugged and the water lapped against me. It stroked me between the legs and the sensation was intensely erotic.

"Would you like to touch yourself now?"

Actually, I'd rather have *him* touch me, but that wasn't the answer he was looking for.

"Yes, sir."

He scooped up another bite and gestured with his fork. "Do it. Make yourself come."

I blushed. And then I started to stroke myself between my thighs.

But...I couldn't do it.

I couldn't bring myself to orgasm with him standing there, watching me as he ate, like this was some sort of amusing dinnertime entertainment.

Nerves made me clumsy and what had started out feeling so incredibly sexy and naughty suddenly felt awkward.

I fumbled with my fingers and although the water was wet and slick against me, it was awkward, sliding my fingers inside myself. I grimaced. The water wasn't enough to make it easy.

As though he'd sensed what was happening, Dominic put the plate down and came to me. He knelt beside the tub and studied me. "Shall I make you come, Aleena? Would you like that?"

Speechless, I nodded, gazing up at him.

"How do you ask me then?"

"Please make me come, sir."

He pretended to consider it. "I might. But if I do, you'll have to do something else for me. Because you teased me and made me think you'd touch yourself and play with yourself until you orgasmed. I wanted to watch you and my cock is still hard from thinking about it. You have to make it up to me. Will you make it up to me, Aleena?"

"Yes, sir." I hesitated and then asked, "What would you like me to do, sir?"

"You won't wear panties to work tomorrow."

"But..."

He shrugged. "Okay. I'm going to get to work." He stood up, his erection clearly pressing against the front of his dress pants.

"Wait!"

He glanced down at me, face hard. "You said you wanted to be my submissive, Aleena. You don't get to tell me to wait."

"I'm sorry, sir." Looking down into the water, I held my breath. The need was still there, throbbing deep, but I knew if he left, I wouldn't be able to get myself off.

His hand tangled in my hair and he tugged. “What would you like to ask me?”

“Please make me come...sir. And I won’t wear panties tomorrow.”

He smiled down at me and returned to where he'd been kneeling.

As he slid his hand down into the water, it dawned on me...*I’m in so much trouble...*

Chapter 8

Dominic

I'd developed a new favorite past time and that was anything I could do to steal Aleena's panties.

So far, I'd confiscated four pair.

She was out shopping for more even now.

Being away from her was both good and bad. It let me focus on work and all the projects that routinely crammed my brain. At the same time, it let my mind stray back to her and the things I wanted to do to her—and the things I wasn't sure I'd ever get to do.

I was becoming obsessed.

The ticking of the clock was driving me crazy and I ended up locking myself in my office where I heard nothing but the sound of my own breathing and the flipping of pages and the occasional chime of my email as I dealt with one project, then moved to another, before getting distracted by something else entirely. It was chaos and it was insanity and I thrived on it.

The sound of the front door opening, followed by a familiar voice was a welcome respite.

“Hello!”

“Back here, Fawna!”

There was a low, bleat of a cry and something that was both panic and curiosity bled through me. “You brought the little guy, didn’t you?”

She came through my door just as I rose from my desk.

Fawna paused there, grinning at me. “Well, it’s not like I was going to leave him with a babysitter. He’s too young.”

Cautious, I edged closer.

“He’s not going to bite, Dominic,” she said, her voice full of laughter.

I cocked a brow. “I’ve seen babies. They do bite. It’s that teething thing.”

“He won’t be teething for a long time.” She put the car seat down and whipped off a soft, fuzzy blue blanket, revealing a wide-eyed, red-cheeked little baby who looked almost nothing like the fragile little guy I’d last seen hooked up to a tube and machines that did all his breathing for him.

“Wow,” I murmured. “He’s gotten bigger.”

“They do that.” With the same competence she always displayed, Fawna undid the straps that held him in place and hefted her grandson out, cradling him in her arms before turning to me, displaying him. “Don’t worry. I won’t ask you to hold him. I can already see the panic in your eyes.”

"I'm not panicking," I lied.

"Sure." She gave me a knowing smile. She sat down and I took the chair across from her.

"You look..." I paused and then sighed. "You look happy, Fawna."

"I am." She smiled at me. "Thank you, Dominic. For everything."

Unable to figure out how to respond to that, I just nodded.

"You look rather happy yourself."

Rising, I moved over to the window. I slid my hands into my pockets and rocked back. I didn't know what to say or how to handle that. I couldn't lie to her. I could lie to a lot of people, but never Fawna. So I didn't bother. "I'm sleeping with Aleena."

The silence was so abrupt and brittle, I almost cringed.

Finally, Fawna cleared her throat and then softly said, "Dammit."

I turned to look at her, but she wasn't looking at me. She fiddled around in the bag next to her and I watched as she pulled out a bottle, popped it open somehow and then shook it. She slid out of the room and I heard a faint beep a moment later. A couple of minutes passed and she returned, the bottle popped in the baby's mouth.

She sat down and then before I even had a chance to brace myself, she pinned me with a hard, direct stare.

"Why?"

Not exactly what I'd been expecting.

I could have said a hundred things and I would have said any of them if it had been anybody but Fawna. This was the woman who had basically become my mother, in all the ways that counted. Seriously, was there a guy out there who'd be comfortable telling his mother something like...*looking at her makes my dick hard and my brain go blank*?

Because that was the first thing that came to mind.

I couldn't comfortably say that. And I wouldn't have said that to anybody—not about Aleena.

"Isn't that my business?"

Fawna's eyes narrowed. "Dominic, I like that girl."

"I like her too." That was another one of the things I could have said. Should I have started off with that one? I shoved a hand through my hair and stood up to pace.

I hadn't even taken three steps before Fawna's voice stopped me. "Then why are you doing this? Complicating things?"

"How is it complicating things?" I snapped and glared at her. "Hell, you're the one who told me she could be good for me."

"Yes! Professionally. This isn't professional." The baby in her arms squawked and Fawna sighed, bringing him to her shoulder. She hummed to him in that way women seemed to always know how to do. As he calmed, Fawna rose and started to move.

Not exactly pacing, but swaying. "Dominic, this isn't smart. Surely you have to know that. You've never done this before. Why start now?"

"Because nobody ever got to me like she does," I answered bluntly.

That made Fawna turn back to me and the look in her eyes was faintly surprised.

She slowly returned to the couch, still rocking the baby.

I glanced at him, then away. Then back. "He's asleep."

"They do that too," she said, her voice wry. She settled him down in his car seat and then moved it to the floor. A couple of moments passed and I said nothing. She was thinking, but I recognized this mood. She was...considering.

Finally, she sighed and looked back at me.

"I don't think it's a good idea to get involved with an employee, you know that." She laughed and shook her head, brushing her hair back from her face. It donned on me then that she'd left it down. I don't know if I'd ever seen her looking so casual. I studied her more closely and realized the subtle differences were numerous. Her hair was down, her make-up a little lighter, but brighter. She wore blue jeans and a bright blue sweater. And tennis shoes. I'd never seen her in tennis shoes.

But everything that made her Fawna? None of that had changed.

She still cut right to the chase.

"I think you probably know it's not a good idea

too," she added, her eyes watchful.

"It's not like I planned it." I felt defensive now. "Hell, you're the one who brought her to that so-called second interview."

"I know. And I'm sitting here now, talking to you and I realize you seem...happy. Dominic, I don't know when I've ever seen you look happy." She held out a hand to me. "Not for real."

I'd never been able to refuse such a simple gesture from her, so I took it and when she tugged me down to sit, I accepted. The scrutiny she subjected me to was thorough and intense. Whatever she saw made her face relax.

"Maybe she is good for you." Fawna nodded. Then she pointed a finger at me. "But you better be careful, Dominic. Don't you hurt that girl. I mean it."

***

Later, after she'd left, I wandered the empty silence of the penthouse.

Aleena had sent me a text and told me that Molly had wanted to meet for lunch. Did I need her for anything?

My instinctive response had been *Yes*.

So I'd told her she was welcome to take all the time she needed.

Better that she not know that I was starting to need her for all sorts of things. I already had a list of questions I needed her to answer and another list of things I had no idea what I needed, but I knew she'd have the answers tucked inside that beautiful head.

Then there were all things unrelated to work that I needed from her.

Need...

It was something I wasn't comfortable with.

I didn't like *needing* anything. I didn't like *depending* on anybody.

It took me back to ugly places and ugly times when I'd had to rely on somebody for every last fucking thing—from the very air I breathed to the food in my belly to even being allowed to take a piss.

I can't breathe...memory shrieked through my brain and I drilled the heel of my hand into my eye socket, trying to expunge the voices. Mine. His.

You want me to let you breathe? Then beg me.

Please...please...Lungs burning, screaming. Hands on my throat.

What will you do...?

"Dominic! I'm home!"

The sound of her voice jerked me out of the past. That need, the one I'd been denying screamed that I go to her.

Instead, I braced my hands on the window and leaned forward, staring out the glass over the city.

Maybe I had made a mistake. But it wasn't the employee thing that was starting to worry me.

It was Aleena and how much I was starting to *need* her.

I couldn't do that though.

I couldn’t let myself need anybody or anything.

Chapter 9

Aleena

The man was giving me whiplash.

He was also giving me a headache and what I preferred to think was indigestion rather than the miserable feeling of a broken heart.

He can't be breaking your heart, girl, I thought broodingly. *That would mean you fell in love and we aren't doing that.*

I frowned. *No,* I thought. *We aren't...but I could...*

Miserable, I stared at my agenda without really seeing it. Dominic wasn't here. I'd come in to meet with Amber to go over certain details about *Trouver L'Amour.* She was starting to look for her replacement since she never stayed at the new Winter Corporation businesses long. She would be back to the main offices of Winter Corporation soon enough, but first we needed to find somebody to take over at the dating agency.

I'd been pleasantly surprised, and pleased, when she asked if I'd help her go through the resumes. I really didn't think I was qualified, and told her so, and she'd laughed it off.

"Trust me...you're going to be spending a lot of time here for a while. You have to get along with whoever is sitting in this seat. If you're not happy with her, or him, Dominic won't be happy. So let's just avoid it." She rolled her eyes and sipped from her coffee. "How much time do we have?"

I checked my agenda. "He's doing an interview." I grinned at her.

"Lovely." Amber gave me a solemn look over her coffee cup. "He'll come back ready to bite heads off. He *hates* interviews."

"I've noticed." I paused as I read through one interview and then passed it onto the maybe file. "He's only had me..."

The elevator doors whispered open and the two of us went quiet as a tall, elegant woman stepped through. Professionally cut brown hair and an outfit that cost more than most people made in a month.

"Ms. Rittenour." Amber rose from behind the desk and moved out to greet the other woman. She didn't hold out a hand though.

I wouldn't have either. Something about the icily beautiful woman in front of me made me think the lady would expect you to bow over her hand, not shake it.

Her gaze flicked to me and then back to Amber.

"Is he in?"

"I'm afraid not." Amber's voice was polite. Perfectly polite. And...that was it.

Okay. I'd gotten to know Amber over the past few weeks and that tone already had me cautious. Amber was an absolute doll from everything I could tell. If she was using that tone, that could only mean a few things—things *could* get ugly, things were likely to *get* ugly or they already were. She had a different manner for dealing with things if everything was either moving on track or just not going her way. I'd figured *that* out the first week of working here.

Since I didn't know which way this would go, I started gathering up the resumes and slipping them back into the file. I didn't want to be here when whatever it was happened.

"When will he be returning to the office?"

"I'm afraid I don't know, Ms. Rittenour." Amber turned to me. There was a message in her eyes and I read it loud and clear. *He isn't going to be in.*

I inclined my head and thought back. I knew the name. If I was right, this was Penelope Rittenour. I'd been fielding calls and emails from her for the past couple of weeks, and Amber was right. Dominic wasn't very likely to be in.

Or at least, he wouldn't *want* to be in for her.

"I can consult his schedule and see if he'll be available any time soon, Ms...?" I purposefully left out her last name, as if she hadn't been important enough for me to remember.

"Rittenour," she bit off. "It's Penelope Rittenour." She raked me with a dismissive look. "And you are...?"

I moved out from behind the desk. I don't know what drove me. Maybe it was that dismissive look or maybe it was the way she spoke to me in almost the same tone Jacqueline St. James-Snow had used. But I found myself holding out my hand. "I'm Aleena Davison, Dominic's personal assistant."

One thing I knew about the New York elite by now. *Most* of them wouldn't be caught dead actually being rude. Not in front of witnesses at least. They were more about the subtle insults.

After a hard stare at me, Penelope reached out and took my hand. I couldn't call it a shake. She merely rested her hand in mine for the briefest pause. When she pulled away, I could see her resisting the urge to wipe her hand and I resisted an urge myself. *Don't worry,* I wanted to say. *Being middle class and biracial isn't contagious, honey.*

"His assistant." Penelope flicked her fingers together, almost as if she was trying to dislodge the feel of the unwashed masses from her skin.

I bit the inside of my cheek to keep a sneer from forming.

"Yes." I pretended to consider it and glanced over at Amber. "I think it's been...oh, about six weeks or so since I've started. Does that sound right?"

"Yes." She nodded, giving me a small smile. "We're very happy with Ms. Davison."

"Lovely." Penelope looked bored. "I imagine it's...pleasant work, keeping up with a man like Dominic." She arched a perfectly plucked eyebrow and smiled at me, but there was nothing polite in the smile. It was one-hundred percent, grade-A bitch. "His mother and I had lunch the other day. Just chatting, of course. We get together every so often, have been friends for years. She's...well." She shrugged. "Dominic and I have always been close, so I'm glad..."

The elevator doors whispered open, all but soundless.

I had my teeth clenched together so hard, it nearly gave me a headache and that promise of a headache sprang into full, throbbing existence when Dominic stepped out.

Penelope gave both Amber and I cutting looks before she turned and strode toward him. "Dominic!" She had her hands stretched out. "Really, you need to hire better help..." She infused laughter into the words, but the spite was clear, all the same. "Neither of these...ladies seemed to think you'd be back for hours."

"I wasn't supposed to be," he said, his voice dark. He flicked Amber and me a look before settling his gaze on Amber. "Amber, contact the florist and send something to..."

Penelope was stroking a hand up and down his arm.

I was going to throw up.

Dominic looked down at her and she gave him a

saccharine smile. He gave her a polite one back and then strode over to stand closer to me. “Dammit. I can’t even remember where we were,” he said.

“Is everything okay, Dominic?” I asked guardedly. He looked...odd.

He shook his head. “We were having sushi. Mr. Kim, his assistant and the translator, plus another man...fuck...” He shoved a hand through his hair. “I should have had you there because we ended up covering a lot more than I’d planned and now my head is shot. Anyway, the translator had a reaction to something she ate and they had to call an ambulance.”

“A reaction?”

Penelope clearly felt left out. “Dominic, I was wondering if—”

“A few minutes, Penelope.” He flicked a hand in her direction, the tone and gesture clearly dismissive. “My phone’s busted. I dropped it during the commotion and it was smashed. Order me a new one and make sure it’s set up.”

I nodded and turned over my phone, watching as he pulled up the agenda. “Yeah, that’s the place,” he muttered. He fired off the name to Amber. “Find out where the ambulance would have taken the woman who had the allergic reaction.” He bent over and wrote her name down. “Send flowers. And then send a case of scotch to Mr. Kim’s hotel.”

“I’d think she’d need it more,” I muttered as I mentally ran down all the things I'd need to do to get Dominic's phone set up.

He flashed me a grin despite the clear stress lines on his face. "She's alive because of him. He figured out what was happening, knocked me out of my chair and laid her out flat, bellowed at me to call *911* and then demanded that I find an epi-pen."

I blinked, trying to imagine the diminutive man I knew to be Mr. Kim barking demands at anybody, much less Dominic. Amber seemed to be picturing the same thing and I saw her fighting the same smile I was.

"She's going to be fine, though, right?" I asked.

"I hope so." He blew out a breath and then finally looked over at Penelope, his polite, professional mask back in place. He gestured toward his office. "Why don't we step inside, Penelope?"

He nodded at me. "Aleena, take care of the phone, please. Oh, if either of you hear from Mr. Kim, set up another meeting whenever it's convenient for him. A man capable of making decisions like that is definitely a man I want to do business with." He reached into his pocket and pulled out a business card, turning it over to me. "Start researching his company, Aleena. Get some background information."

I looked down at the card as he closed the door, locking himself and Penelope inside.

The name card made my eyes widen.

"Ah..." Heat flooded my face.

Amber glanced up at me, then reached over and plucked the card out of my hand.

A moment later, we were both giggling like a

couple of silly teenagers. Maybe it was some sort of hysterical distraction, but I'd much rather be thinking about quiet, reserved Mr. Kim, who apparently was the head of a massive sex toy operation, than the fact that Dominic was inside his office...with the rich, beautiful Penelope Rittenour.

Chapter 10

Dominic

"You know, if you would like some assistance finding some quality help, I'd be happy to..." Penelope paused and when I looked at her, she smiled. "Well, I have some experience in this area."

Frowning, I asked, "What area?" What was she talking about?

She gestured back toward the door. "Your new personal assistant doesn't seem to have much experience, Dominic. She's certainly attractive, but wherever did you find her?"

"I didn't." Folding my arms my chest, I gave her a hard stare. "Fawna did, and I have to say, Aleena already has my life compartmentalized and organized down to the last dotted *i* and the last crossed *t*. I'm not sure how you could possibly hope to find anybody who could do any better—especially not if they're expected get along with me twenty-four seven." I surprised myself by the extent to which I'd defended her.

Penelope's eyes widened. "She..." She pursed her lips. "She lives in Fawna's apartment?"

"Where else?" I shrugged and moved back to my desk, trying to make it seem like thinking about Aleena living just down the hall from me wasn't distracting. It had been an insane day, and the last thing I wanted to do was deal with Penelope, but she was here. Gesturing to the seat across from my desk, I gave her a smile she would have recognized if she knew me at all well. It was the *let's get this over so you can get out* smile.

Penelope must have read it as my *Please...make a move* smile because she came around the desk and leaned a hip against it. "I've missed seeing you, Dominic," she said.

She lifted a hand and, instinctively, I froze.

Most people would recognize when somebody didn't want a physical touch.

Penelope, however, was one of those people who couldn't imagine why somebody *wouldn't* want her touch and she continued on her course, stroking her hand through my hair. I tolerated it because I refused to let her see me jerking away and recoiling. That would look too much like weakness.

Penelope was one of the women who fell outside my normal categories for women. I wouldn't fuck her, but I hadn't initiated a social relationship, so I hadn't explained my rules for either of those two categories.

My rules were simple in either case. For social

events, I made sure the groundwork was set before we went anywhere. *This isn't love. I'm not going to fall in love with you. I'm not interested in a romantic relationship so I'd like to avoid things that go with them. I'll hold your arm as we go to and from events, but beyond that, let's keep all physical contact to a minimum.*

Penelope seemed to think I might be a catch or some bullshit.

That wasn't going to happen.

Perhaps it was time to explain that.

But as I rose from the chair, my thoughts wandered, shifted, then slid to Aleena. If she'd reached up and brushed my hair back, I wouldn't mind. Those little casual touches others engaged in...well, she didn't do them, but I was starting to wish she would. I was starting to miss the fact that she didn't.

I was starting to regret things and miss them and want them. And it would only get worse, I knew, because as I'd already admitted to myself, I was coming to need her.

Two seconds from explaining the ugly facts of Dominic Snow to Penelope Rittenour, I stopped.

The phone rang before I could think things through a second time and I moved to answer it. I almost didn't when I saw my mother's name flash up on the display, but in the end, I closed my hand around the receiver and lifted it to my ear.

If I didn't talk to her, eventually, she might try to contact Aleena.

I wouldn't subject Aleena to that.

"Hello, Mom."

From the corner of my eye, I saw Penelope move into the seat behind my desk. I set my jaw and gave her a hard look. She smiled innocently at me and crossed her legs.

Damn, she was annoying. Sucking in a breath through my teeth, I turned my back.

"Darling. How are you?"

"I'm well enough." I didn't bother to ask how she was.

"I..." After a moment, she tried haltingly to break the silence. "I assume you're..."

"Aleena still works for me if that's what you're fumbling around to ask, Mom. Nothing has changed. If you're disappointed..." I let the words trail off. I wouldn't lie and offer a false apology. And there was no way in hell I was going to tell her the one thing that had changed.

"You're still angry with me." She sounded almost amused.

"What clued you in?"

"Really, Dominic," she said, her voice chiding. "There's no reason for you to be so rude."

"Of course." I nodded and gazed outside. "That's *your* domain, isn't it, Mom?"

Her harsh intake of breath was audible. "Dominic, I am *sorry* if I upset you."

"And her?" I asked, gazing restlessly out over the city skyline.

"I...whatever do you mean?"

"I wasn't the one you insulted, Mom."

"Well. Of course. Listen, Dominic. I think this would be best if we discussed it in person. Can we...can we talk? Please?"

Closing my eyes, I blocked out the entreating tone of her voice. I knew better.

"Dominic, I feel terrible about Friday. I made several missteps and I'd like to...well, make amends. Can you please come? It's been so long since the two of us have even had any real time together."

I mentally snorted. She made missteps, yeah. I almost pointed out that her missteps had mostly been with Aleena and both of us had screwed up there. But one thing was certain. My mother needed to understand that she would never make those missteps with Aleena again. And as much as I hated her machinations, Jacqueline St. James-Snow was my mother. She'd been the one to stand by me, to make sure I got help, care...everything. After.

I didn't like having a wall between us even if our relationship was stilted at best.

"Fine, Mom," I said softly. "When?"

"Tomorrow night?" The hesitant tone in her voice was unlike her.

Maybe she was trying.

"Okay." I realized I was nodding to myself. A few moments later, I turned and stared at Penelope. She was still in my chair.

"That's my desk," I pointed out.

"Oh." She gave me a wide, startled look. "I'm sorry...I just...well. I was trying to give you some privacy, Dominic."

I glanced pointedly at the big doors that opened to the outer offices and then back at her. She colored slightly, but said nothing.

"What can I do for you, Penelope?" I asked, fighting the urge to sigh.

Penelope beamed at me.

"I think I want to try the service out."

***

There are some things a rich bastard can do and not worry about.

There are some things a rich bastard can do and the shit will hit the fan and he can shrug it off.

The one thing a rich bastard can't do it is tell a client—no, *potential* client—like Penelope Rittenour that I'd love to have her and then pass her off to one of his associates.

Especially as she'd made it clear that she'd come here specifically looking for me. I'd tried to be diplomatic and explain that in order to give her the best service, I'd really need to give her to my best people, but she hadn't gone for it. I was one hell of a businessman and I knew it. I could sell shit to some of the savviest people out there and make them think they were buying diamonds, but Penelope hadn't gone for it and in the end, I'd agreed to work with her. The last thing I needed was for her to go out there and start muttering to her friends that the company wasn't delivering what I'd promised. *Her* friends were the clientele I needed in here, which meant I needed her happy.

Which meant I might have already screwed myself.

She wasn't looking for a match through the company, though, and I knew it.

She was looking for a match with me.

After I'd escorted her to the elevator, I locked myself in my office, not speaking to either Amber or Aleena.

Hands behind my back, I stared outside, but I didn't see the skyline of the city where I'd lived all my life and I couldn't admire the view I'd chosen to make my own when I'd set up my offices.

No, mentally, I was seeing two women.

Two beautiful women.

The one I'd just escorted from my office and the one who was only a few feet away, in my outer office.

One, I couldn't stand. I could barely tolerate Penelope's presence. She was shallow and vapid and vain and could hardly hold a conversation that didn't revolve around fashion and society, which was pathetic, because I knew she had excelled in college, but she'd focused all that brainpower on things she felt mattered. Clothing and the charities she felt were worthy of attention...I think right now it had something to do with a rare orchid I'd never heard of. Last year, it was knitting sweaters for penguins. When I'd asked her about the penguins, she'd stared at me as if I'd lost my mind.

The next time I asked her about the orchids, I had no doubt it would be the same.

She'd asked once if her family and mine could work together on a charitable cause and I'd said I'd consider it, then I mentioned I was looking into partnering with a group I'd heard of in Africa. I'd showed her some of the information I'd had. Her face had tightened.

Starving children with bloated bellies was too unseemly for Penelope Rittenour. She'd asked if perhaps I'd be interested in arctic foxes.

No. I hadn't been interested in arctic foxes.

Penelope Rittenour was beautiful and from one of the most powerful families in the northeast. The Rittenour's could trace their roots back for centuries, and she was happy to tell you that.

She'd make the perfect society wife.

A faint laugh echoed from the outer office and I closed my eyes. Bracing my forearm against the window, I rested my brow against it and let my thoughts wander to the other beautiful woman...the one I couldn't stop thinking about. The one just a few feet away. The one I was coming to crave like a drug. The one I wanted to see bent over before me, stretched out beneath me, standing in front of me with her arms bound overhead.

Aleena.

I could come to need her—was already so close to it.

I'd forced myself to keep my distance this week

and it hadn't lessened that need at all. I'd dealt with it, tolerated it. I'd even visited my club briefly, although it had done nothing for me. The boredom I'd felt too often these days had only intensified and even the thought of touching one of the Subs who visited, looking for a brief visit from an unattached Dom like myself, had left me feeling faintly disgusted.

"Stop it. You don't owe her a damn thing," I said, anger burning inside me.

I couldn't owe her. That would mean I'd committed or let myself come to need her or care more than I'd let myself allow. We called it a relationship, but we hadn't set any terms.

There was a knock at the door and I lowered my arm, took a moment to smooth my suit—and my expression.

Without turning to the door, I said, "Come in."

"Dominic?"

"Yes, Ms. Davison?"

There was a pause and I heard the stiffness in her tone when she responded, "Mr. Kim is on the phone. He wanted to thank—"

"Please send the call on through, Ms. Davison." I turned toward the desk and flicked her a look. "I'm having dinner with my mother tomorrow. There's a wine she enjoys...I can't remember the name. Fawna might have it in her notes. If she doesn't, give her a call. She'll remember it."

I reached for the phone.

"Have I done something wrong?" Her voice was

quiet but steady. “You told me I had to be honest with you. Don't I deserve the same courtesy?”

I should have known better than to get involved with her. She wouldn’t cling. I already knew that. But she wasn’t going to quietly fade back into the background, either. She would call me on my shit.

Fawna had warned me about getting involved, but the warning had come too late. I'd already been in too deep.

“No, Ms...” I sighed and looked at her, saw the dull flush of color on her cheeks, the pain flashing across her eyes. “No, Aleena. My mother wants to make amends. And things are complicated. I need to think.”

“Of course, Mr. Snow.” She inclined her head and turned to go. There was no animosity in her words, but no warmth either.

She knew I wasn't being completely honest.

“Aleena—”

“Mr. Kim is waiting,” she said. Then she closed the door.

Chapter 11

Aleena

I'd found the wine Dominic had requested.

He'd taken it with him when he left for the office that morning and I'd stayed home to work in the home office.

We'd fallen into something of a routine and Mondays, Wednesdays and Thursdays were the days I normally went into the office with him unless there was something specific going on and he requested that I go in too.

Since he hadn't made that request, I'd already busied myself at my desk, dressed in my 'home' work attire, hoping he wouldn't make any changes to our 'routine' and he hadn't.

I was glad.

When the door shut behind him, I kept working a good twenty minutes, what I considered my safety zone, because he sometimes forgot things when I didn't go in with him. No, he *often* forgot things.

It hadn't taken me long to understand just why

the man had a personal assistant. He was sharp as a whip, but he had too many thoughts inside his head and no sense of organization. I'd once mentioned it and he'd shrugged it off. *That's why I had Fawna...and now, you.* I'd known enough kids back in Iowa who had ADHD to figure that was probably the case.

Once those twenty minutes ticked away, I let myself breathe out a quiet sigh of relief and leaned back, covering my face with my hands.

I hadn't been able to drop my guard at all since he'd made that announcement yesterday.

His mother wanted to make amends?

"Like hell." The waspish note in my voice didn't go unnoticed by me, but fuck it. I figured I had every right to feel waspish. And bitchy. And pissed off. Maybe she did want to, but that wasn't the reason Dominic was acting so stand-offish. He wasn't being honest with me. Even after he'd made me promise to be that way with him.

Feeling like I was going to come out of my skin, I got up and started to pace. Back and forth, I went across the office.

There was work waiting for me on the desk, but I'd been unable to sleep most of the night, so I'd taken care of probably a third of the things in my inbox already. Dominic's ridiculous social calendar was now updated, save for a few things I needed to confirm with him. I knew better than email over those.

The phone rang and I drifted over to look at it,

considered not answering it, but I had come to take my job too seriously. I couldn't let my personal life interfere. With a sigh, I picked it up.

"Snow residence, this is Aleena. How may I help you?"

There was a faint pause, followed by a sniff.

I rolled my eyes. *Spare me.*

"Aleena."

The way the woman drew my name out told me everything I needed to know. I didn't even look at the caller ID to see if I was correct. I did, however, hit the button that would allow me to record the conversation. Call me suspicious, but I didn't trust her.

"Ms. Rittenour. How are you?"

She didn't even have the courtesy to respond.

"Fetch Dominic."

"I'm afraid I can't do that." I sat down in his chair and fought the urge to breathe in the scent that immediately surrounded me. Picking up a pen, I started to sketch out Penelope Rittenour—as an Afghan hound. The long, gleaming coat...er...hair, the elegant long face...

She'd make a lovely Afghan hound, and she'd probably be more pleasant too. Those were beautiful and very sweet dogs.

"I need to speak to Dominic," she snapped. "Put him on the phone *now* or I'll have your fucking job."

I pulled the receiver away and eyed it narrowly. Then I put it back to my ear. "I'm uncertain as to how you can have me fired simply because Mr. Snow isn't here at the same time you called, Ms. Rittenour. I'd be happy to take a message though."

Her hiss of breath was audible. Then, coolly, she said, "Give me his cell phone."

"Now that would likely get me fired. I'm afraid I can't pass out personal information without Mr. Snow giving me the authorization first."

"I'm a close *personal* friend."

"Then I'm certain you understand that he's a very private man. Once he tells me it's okay to give you his cell phone number, I'll be happy to do so, Ms. Rittenour." I added a little diamond collar to the dog's neck and diamond earrings. She had Penelope's big eyes and thick eyelashes and maybe I was being catty, but I made sure that snide light shown in her eyes. I used to love to do caricatures, but I never had the time anymore. This was fun.

"Dominic is going to hear of your rudeness...what was it, *Aleena*?"

"Yes, Ms. Rittenour. If you like, I'd be happy to call him as soon as we hang up and let him know about our discussion." I paused and then added, "His home office is set up to record all incoming calls. Shall I play the conversation back for him to ensure he knows everything we discussed?"

There was a long, weighted pause and then she said, "You think you're smart, don't you?"

"Of course not, Ms. Rittenour. I'm just trying to be helpful."

She hung up.

I leaned back, stared at my image of Penelope as

an Afghan hound. If I were trying to be accurate, I would have drawn her as a succubus. Out to drain the life out of whatever man she'd set her sights on, and it so happened to be Dominic she'd chosen as her prey. I shouldn't care, not after he was making it clear that, no matter what we'd said, he was going to keep me at arm's length.

I pulled the sheet of paper free, and then, to be safe, I tugged out the next two and put them in the cross-cut shredder.

That done, I sent a text to Dominic.

Ms. Rittenour called. She would like to speak with you and she'd also like your cellphone number. I'm afraid she's not happy with me. I wouldn't give her the number without your permission and that made her angry. Shall I give her the number? Please advise.

I double-checked to make sure the phone call had been recorded. I'd told a white lie. He didn't record *all* calls. I think it was illegal to record things without permission, but he did get a lot of business calls—those he *did* get permission for and it was simply because he didn't like forgetting details.

I suspected he also had less than pleasant phone calls. Perhaps calls like mine, where people tried to levy threats against him, although I don't know who'd be stupid enough to threaten a man like Dominic. Blackmail, maybe. The ability to record anybody that stupid would be useful.

I'd never asked. I hoped he wouldn't be mad, but if he was...

I sighed.

His response came back before I made it back to my desk.

Don't worry about Penelope. I'll get back with her when I see her or she can call the office and leave a message here. And no, please don't give her my number. You did the right thing. Thank you.

Biting my lip, I considered it a moment and then sent him one more message.

She tells me that she going to have me fired since I didn't give her the number. She'll be sure to tell you how rude I was. She was even more pissed off when I mentioned that you have your phone set up to record incoming calls. I might have told a little white lie there. I'm sorry.

This time, the response was immediate.

Good thinking and don't be sorry. Don't worry, either. You're not fired, Aleena. Why don't you take the day off? You could probably use a break. You've done nothing but work all week. Take the day off. Go see Molly. Go shopping. I'll deal with Penelope.

I blew out a relieved breath. If he'd been angry, he would have said something. He was holding back, but he wasn't being rude.

I responded with a quick thank you and then studied my pile of work. I could always put in a few hours tomorrow, but I really could use a break. I had been working a lot lately.

Chapter 12

Dominic

"Really, Dominic. You let your *employee* talk that way to friends?"

I looked up over the rim of my wineglass toward my mother. Slowly, I put it down and then got up, heading over the bar. I poured myself a double of Macallan. It was twenty-one years old and I brought it to my nose, breathed it in and forced my shoulders to relax for a moment as I took one small sip.

"Dominic..."

At my mother's chiding voice, I turned to face her.

Mom was sitting next to Penelope and I had to fight not to clench my jaw at the sight of her. They'd both been there waiting when I arrived and I'd almost left.

My mother had set this up. I had no doubt about it.

I looked back at Penelope to answer her

question even though it was probably meant to be rhetorical. "Well, my mother talks to my employees in a far worse manner," I said, shrugging. "All Aleena did was follow my instructions and not give out my personal information without my permission."

I took a small sip of scotch as my mother's face went red, then white. While she struggled to come up with a response, I added, "Should I discipline her for it, Mother?"

Her eyes widened and, for a moment, I thought she was going to choke on her drink.

Penelope, unaware of the double meaning, laid a hand on my mother's arm. "Jacqueline, I'm sure the girl didn't mean to be so rude," she said, a gentle—and completely false—smile on her face.

"She wasn't." Tired of the bullshit, I headed back to the table and eyed the remains of the dinner. Étienne, my mother's chef, had prepared a wonderful meal. He always did. But it had tasted like sawdust and it now sat like a rock in my stomach. Slumping in the chair, I eyed Penelope for a moment. I was too pissed off at my mother's obvious machinations, and Penelope's manipulations, to care if she decided to fuck with *Trouver L'Amour*. If she did, I'd just deal with it. It wasn't like I didn't know how to play the game too. I was sure most people wouldn't have a problem seeing Penelope as a conniving jealous bitch.

When Penelope started to argue, I cut her off. "I listened to your phone call, Penelope. You called, demanded to speak with me and she said she couldn't put me on the phone. You told her to either do it or you'd have her *fucking* job. She said she couldn't get me on the phone since I wasn't there and, rightly, it wasn't likely she could be fired over that. Then you demanded my phone number and when she wouldn't give it to you, you yelled at her *again*."

With a cold smile, I added, "She texted me right away to let me know you'd called and asked if she should give you my number."

"Tattling on me, is she?" Penelope's cheeks were pale, save for two red spots riding high on her cheeks.

Now it was my mother's turn to reach over and pat Penelope's hand. "Simply covering herself. That's what girls..."

My gaze left Penelope and went straight to my mother.

Jacqueline cleared her throat. "That's what a professional is supposed to do in this case, Penelope. Check with her superior and make sure she'd taken the right steps. Isn't that right, Dominic?"

"Yes."

Penelope continued to stare at me. "Then why didn't she contact me back with your phone number?"

"Because I told her not to." I tossed the rest of my Macallan back and debated on another. I wanted it. Almost craved it. And because I did, I deliberately pushed the glass away. Self-control. Denial. Always.

"But I..." She licked her lips and, for the first time that evening, she looked uncertain. Her gaze fell away and she stared at the window that faced out over the elegance of the gardens. They were lit with small white bulbs threaded through the trees and carefully placed lights on the ground. "Dominic, I wanted to speak with you."

"Then you could have called the office or left a message. I'm a busy man, Penelope. I don't have time for idle chit-chat. Surely you know that."

My mother's laugh, light and practiced, broke the strained silence. "Of course you're a busy man. Penelope, Dominic...this is all such a silly matter, and over a new personal assistant." Her gaze darted to me and then away. "I'm sure Aleena is doing the best she can and she handled the matter as she felt was best, yes?"

"Of course." Penelope gave me a tremulous smile.

I didn't smile back.

The way Mom acted, you'd think I had.

She clapped her hands. "Wonderful. We won't speak of it again. Why don't we retire to the drawing room?"

I managed not to roll my eyes.

The *drawing room*...where she could have another drink without looking like she was tossing it back.

***

"I am sorry, Dominic."

Mother spoke to me softly as Penelope played the piano.

I didn't look at her. "Are you?"

"You know I am." She laid a hand on my arm. "I hate to have anything come between us and this has."

"Then why are you apologizing to me instead of the woman you insulted?" Now I turned my head and stared at her.

"I..." Her hand fluttered up to her throat, then back down to her drink. Finally, she took a sip of her cognac and sat there, head cocked as she listened to the lovely strains drifting from the piano.

It might have been Beethoven. I liked music well enough, but I'd never focused on it as much as my parents would have liked.

"Lovely," she called out as Penelope brought the music to a close. "Can you play another?"

Yes, don't overhear something unpleasant, Penelope. I smirked and settled more comfortably into the couch, staring up at the mural painted on the ceiling.

"How did I insult her, Dominic? Surely she realizes you're from different worlds."

A headache started to pulse behind my brows.

When I didn't answer, she sighed. "I know you think I'm terribly unfair about classes and money, but she'd *never* fit in here. It's just not money—"

"She's not white."

I said it loud enough that Penelope heard and

the music clattered to a halt, a horrified expression on her face. I stood up and strode out of the room. Penelope stared at me and Mom followed.

Fortunately, she was the only one.

"Surely you're not implying that I..." She made a face like I'd shoved a lemon in her mouth. Then, lowering her voice, she added in a hushed tone, "I certainly have no *issue* with her being...being...*ethnic*."

"She's mixed, Mom," I said, turning to face her. Crossing my arms over my chest, I gave her a hard look. "I believe one of the PC terms is *biracial*. Her mom's black. Her dad is white. She's from a nice, middle class family out of Iowa. As she pointed out, she wasn't plucked from one of the zoos here in New York."

"I hardly implied she *was*!"

She looked so offended that I almost laughed.

Jabbing a finger at her, I said, "If I'd had a white woman there with me, you wouldn't have felt the need to point out that I could find *exotic* sex anywhere. Yeah, I get that we don't come from the same world...although...you know what? For all *I* know, my parents *were* middle class and maybe *they* are from Iowa. Or Detroit. For all I know, my real mother was some hooker from Harlem."

"Dominic!" She jerked her head back, covering her mouth. She looked like I'd slapped her.

Guilt and misery flooded me and I swore. "Fuck...Mom. I'm sorry. I...I don't want to hurt you, but I want to know more about where I came from and every time you throw class up at me, it reminds me about how little I do know. But that's not what this is about."

"Then what is it?" she asked, her voice stiff.

"It's about the fact that you don't even see what you are," I said softly. I looked at her and shrugged. "But I can't really blame you. I didn't see it either. I didn't see what I was. Aleena had to point it out. Just because someone isn't wearing a white hood doesn't mean they aren't racist."

"I'm not a racist." Jacqueline St. James-Snow drew her shoulders back and glared down her nose at me, which was saying something since I towered over her.

"Yeah?" I cocked an eyebrow. "Okay. If Penelope was black, would you be so eager to push her at me?"

Her gaze fell away. Almost immediately, her eyes came back and she gave me a polite smile. "Of course. I've chosen not to see color."

"You don't see color, huh? That's a load of bullshit. If you don't see *color*, sounds to me like you've chosen not to see *people* of color. But what do I know...I'm just your rich white son. People like us? We'll never have to deal with people looking past us or through us simply because we're not white enough. Guess we're lucky."

I pushed past her.

"Dominic, wait."

I shook my head. "It's late. I'm tired." I paused, though, and looked back at her. "I do love you, you know. You're my mother and you have always been there, even when I wasn't an easy kid. But I need to know who I am. I'm going to find my birth mother."

She staggered and fell back.

I held out a hand, guilt swamping me.

"Please go," she whispered.

Slowly, I lowered my hand to my side, clenching it into a fist. Moving back out into the hall, I saw Penelope.

She had been standing there, listening the entire time.

Her face was pale, eyes dark.

I simply nodded at her. I didn't think anything else was necessary.

Chapter 13

Dominic

If I were smart, I would have gone to the club.

I was burning inside and the need to empty all the anger, all the frustration was riding me hard.

But I didn't go to the club.

I went home.

Aleena was curled up on the couch in the living room—on *my* couch where I'd first fucked her—watching TV.

She had a glass of wine in her hand when I came inside and she looked over at me, her features curiously blank.

She didn't immediately say anything as I walked behind the couch and put my keys down, my wallet, my cell phone. I hadn't seen her since that morning and it had only been for a few minutes.

I hadn't touched her in several days and my body was screaming for hers. Not for *sex*, not for release, but for *her*.

But just sex wouldn't be enough.

I needed more this time and I wasn't sure she could give me that.

"How was your dinner?" she asked softly, her eyes still on the screen. She'd muted the volume, but still stared at the images flickering across the TV as though they held the answer to life and death.

Crossing to the floor, I sat down in front of her on the coffee table.

Her eyes finally met mine.

"Not good." I thought it through a moment and then said it again. "Not good at all."

I thought about mentioning that my mom had invited Penelope, but decided not to. What was the point?

Her fingers brushed against mine and that light touch was almost too much. I almost grabbed her, almost hauled her off the couch and into my lap. But I didn't.

"I think..." I said slowly. "I think I should go."

"Go?" Aleena said. "But you just got here."

"Yeah." I slid my eyes over her, let my gaze linger on her breasts, then the juncture of her thighs. "And I'm already thinking about how I want to tie you up, how I want to make you beg. I want to feed you my cock and I want to make you plead. I want things you're not ready for, Aleena, but if I don't do something soon, I'm going to explode."

Her mouth fell open and I watched as her breasts rose and fell raggedly. Her skin was flushed. Her bra must've been unlined because her nipples were stabbing into her shirt.

I wanted to pinch them until she was panting and squirming.

“Then do it.”

I jerked my head up at her soft, unsteady suggestion.

“You’re not ready,” I told her. My hands curled into fists, chest tightening as I remembered what had happened when we'd had 'make-up' sex. I'd gone too far, hadn't understood the difference between what I usually did and what I should have done.

“Maybe that’s my decision.” She swallowed and then, after taking a moment to empty her glass of wine, she eased forward and reached out, laying her hands on my thighs.

Fuck.

My cock almost burst through my trousers when she went to her knees in front of me.

“Maybe I’m not ready for everything. But you can teach me. I can learn. That’s what I want.”

I shoved my hand into her hair, tangled it and twisted until her mouth fell open with a pained sigh. “I’m in the mood to make you beg me. I’m in the mood to put bruises and marks on you, Aleena.”

“You want to...” She bit her bottom lip, her eyes on my face. I don't know what she saw there, but something shifted. “You don't want to actually hurt me.”

“No.” I brushed my thumb across the place she'd bitten. I couldn’t hurt her. Not for real. That was one thing I found intolerable—sickening even. But I couldn't think about that, either. Not now. Not with her. "I could never hurt you."

"Then do what you want. Mark me. Bruise me. Make me beg." She pushed up onto her knees and sank her teeth into my lip, sending a sharp pain through me.

Pain that immediately went to my already hard cock. It brought out the monster in me.

"Make me submit, Dominic."

Staring into her pale eyes, I felt the siren's call of her words.

Mark me.

Bruise me.

I wanted it so badly that it hurt. "Are you certain you know what you're asking for?"

"No." The words were soft, almost ragged, her eyes direct. "But I sure as hell want to learn."

I dragged my hand down the front of her shirt, the other still tangled in her hair. I cranked that wrist, holding her head at an angle that had to be uncomfortable. Lowering my mouth to her neck, I raked my teeth across the exposed arch.

I used the other to drag her shirt up.

I sought out one hard, pebbled nipple and I pinched it, squeezing until she whimpered.

"That's the noise I plan on hearing from you. Over and over. I want to hear you whimpering. Begging. Moaning."

I plucked her nipple again and felt her roll her hips toward me.

"And I won't let you come. Not for a long, long

time."

Lifting my head, I stared into her clouded eyes. My whole body was thrumming. I'd never needed anything this badly before.

"When I do, you will be all but ready to die, just for that release." I had to be sure. I couldn't do this if she wasn't, no matter how much I wanted it. "Are you certain?"

She breathed out my name and then demanded, "Will you just do it already?"

Chapter 14

Aleena

The first time I'd seen the bed, I'd thought something was weird about it.

I hadn't been able to figure it out for a while and when I finally had, it was because I'd seen Dominic and another woman...using a similar bed.

Now I was bound to *this* bed, my face away from him.

I was naked.

I could feel him staring at me.

So far, he hadn't touched me other than to secure my bound wrists to the hoop on the bedpost.

I was terrified.

I was aroused.

"Dominic—"

Something came down on my ass and I twisted, crying out in shock. Shocked pain, followed by heat, flooded through me.

What the hell—

Something soft stroked across the side of my breast. "It's a whip. A cat o nine tails, or a cat," Dominic murmured in my ear. "This one is soft, just a few strips of leather mixed in the fur. I've got one that's all leather. I can make it hurt...I can make it whisper soft."

"You..." I swallowed. "You said you didn't do pain, Domin...sir."

"There's pain and there's *pain*, Aleena." He bit down on my earlobe. "What you felt, did it hurt?"

My ass *stung*. But at the same time, I wanted more. There was something deep inside me that craved what he gave me. "It hurt, but..."

"You want more," he finished for me. He stood and put his hand on my shoulder, pressing me back down onto the bed. He trailed the soft strips across my ass.

My eyes closed. "Yes."

"Now, I want you to be silent. If you talk, I won't let you come at all tonight."

I almost told him he was crazy, but I had the feeling he was serious.

Mentally, I braced myself. I wouldn't talk.

I hoped.

He brought the cat down again and I made a strangled sound, but it wasn't an actual word, so I really hoped it didn't count.

Again. Twice more, and my skin was on fire.

"I think your ass has had enough."

I almost breathed a sigh of relief, but then he spoke again.

"Let's try something new."

He grabbed my hips and flipped me over. I gasped as my ass came in contact with the silk sheets.

"Remember, no talking." The leather and fur ghosted over my breasts and my body tightened. "The only word you're allowed to say is your safe word."

No chance of that.

Then he brought the cat down on my breast.

Fuck. I shivered. It hadn't been hard, but definitely more intense than my ass.

He did the other breast this time.

My nipples puckered.

Left, then right.

Heat gathered in my pussy.

Again. And again.

My nipples were throbbing, riding that border between pleasure and pain.

"Spread your legs."

I did and then I almost screamed because this time, the cat reached between my legs, smacking against my lower lips. My mouth opened, but nothing came out but air because he was bringing the cat down again.

And...well, maybe it didn't matter if I made any noise or not now, because it slapped against my clitoris and I came.

I came hard and I came fast, everything going white.

But I didn't make a noise.

When it ended, Dominic was supporting me with one arm around my waist, his lips against my brow. Although his words were stern, I heard a smug smile in them. "I guess I wasn't clear. I thought you were told not to come."

He cupped my chin and drew my face around until I was looking at him. He raised his eyebrow and I opened my mouth to argue. Then, catching myself, I pressed my lips together and glared at him. My heart raced and I wanted to laugh when he grinned at me. Some of the shadows had faded from his face already. Even without the amazing orgasm, the pain I'd felt would've been worth it.

If my arms had been free, I would have grabbed onto him and held on tight.

But he stroked my face and murmured, "You can answer the question, Aleena. But only that."

"I don't recall you telling me I couldn't come, sir. And if you didn't want me to come, then you shouldn't have made me." I said it all very fast.

He chuckled, his eyes shining. Slowly, his arm fell away. "Okay, sweet. This time...don't come. And don't make a noise."

***

I wasn't sure how much more I could take.

Time had lost all meaning and I was now keeping track by how many climaxes he'd denied me.

Five.

Five times he'd brought me to edge and then taken me away.

I was no longer bound to the hoop at the end of the bed that let him twist and turn me. There was no moving this time.

I was tied spread-eagle and facedown, with some sort of wedge under my hips.

And...

I bit my lip to keep from moaning as he pushed a large dildo inside me.

It was larger than he was.

I knew this because he'd told me. Had even given me specific measurements.

"I'll have to go slow," he said, kneeling behind me. He'd slicked it with lube and I knew that because he'd told me. He at least was telling me everything he was doing, so it didn't catch me off guard. "If I don't, I'll hurt you and I don't want that."

Slow was torture.

I felt every excruciating nuance and when he had it nestled completely inside me, he brought the flat of his hand down on my ass and I had to bite my lip to keep from screaming. My arms were actually shaking and I was pretty sure my fingernails were cutting into my palms.

"Now I want you to ride the cock, Aleena."

Confused, I froze. How was I supposed to...?

He stretched out next to me, his back against the headboard. He used one hand to push my hair away.

“Ride it,” he said again.

Slowly, I moved my hips. It didn't really move without any leverage.

“That’s it.” The words were almost a growl.

It was awkward and slow and under his watchful gaze, I felt...embarrassed. But as his eyes slid over me, I didn't see anything but pure lust.

The dildo shifted, pressing against a spot inside me. I unwittingly whimpered.

My gaze flew to his.

He responded with a hard slap on my ass, that made me press my lips down even harder, but said nothing.

Then he reached for the zipper on his trousers.

I watched mesmerized as he pulled himself free and started to stroke himself. I almost forgot to move, but his eyes narrowed and I moved my hips again.

The fat, swollen head of his cock disappeared inside his fist, only to reappear a moment later.

“Do you like watching me do this?” he asked.

I nodded, and then something happened. I twisted slightly to get a better view and the edge of the dildo pressed against the bed, giving me unexpected leverage. My eyes widened as it moved inside me. Oh, fuck.

“That’s good. I like watching you fuck that dildo. I’m thinking I’d like to see you take my cock in your mouth while you ride it.”

I swallowed, remembering the weight of him on my tongue.

"Not tonight, darling." His lips crooked up in a smile. "Someday, I think I'd like to see you take my cock in your ass too."

I shivered.

Now his eyes went dark, locked on my face. "Have you ever thought about that, Aleena? Having a man's dick in your ass?"

I shook my head as heat tripped up and down my spine. My asshole twitched. I was going to explode. Jerking on the bonds that held me in place, I twisted around the dildo. Watching him touch himself, hearing him talk, I didn't care *what* he said. I needed to come.

He laughed softly, reading it on my face. "You'll think about it now, won't you?"

Hell, yes.

He moved then and I barely had time to process it as he pulled the dildo from me, the move so abrupt and savage, it left me reeling...and empty.

Then *he* filled me.

His long, hard body crushed me into the bed. His teeth sank into my neck as he wedged his hand between me and the mattress, his fingers unerringly seeking out my clit as he pounded his cock into me from behind. I could barely breathe and every nerve in my body was on fire. My eyes were squeezed shut, tears rolling down my cheeks as I fought against the impending inferno.

"You can come now, Aleena. My good, beautiful girl...come *now*."

He pinched my clitoris, bit me again and I came

in an explosion of pure pleasure. When I felt him throb inside me, I couldn't stop myself from calling out his name.

It didn't hit us until a few minutes later, when our breathing finally slowed and our pulses returned to normal, that he hadn't worn a condom.

We came out of the shower thirty minutes later, clean but not having spoken. We went into the kitchen first and he poured us each a glass of wine before we went into the living room. I sat next to him on the couch and we each took a drink.

"So...that happened." He set down his glass and wrapped his arms around me, pulling me against him.

I felt a stab of guilt even though I'd been tied up at the time. Literally. "I'm sorry. I know how you feel..."

He silenced me with a kiss and then held me close, his gaze going over my head. "If it was anybody but you, I never would have forgotten. It's never been an issue." He turned his face into my hair and whispered, "What are you doing to me, Aleena?"

I didn't know how to answer because I didn't know what he was doing to me either. I'd never thought I could feel this way about someone.

Instead of trying to explain and risking making things awkward, I slid my hand up and down his arm. "Based on, well, *that*, I'm guessing things didn't go well at your mother's."

He stiffened and for a moment, I thought he'd pull away.

But then he relaxed and from the corner of my eye, I watched as he wrapped a strand of my hair around his finger. “I guess you could say that. They didn’t go well. At all.”

I might have said something else, but then the phone rang.

Frowning, I glanced at it.

It was almost eleven.

“Ignore it,” Dominic said, tugging me back against him. His mouth brushed against mine and his arms tightened. “I’m thinking about rewarding you for doing so well on your first lesson.”

My heart jumped a little. “Really?” I was sore, but I still wanted him.

He smiled.

So did I.

And then we heard the voice coming over the answering machine as the caller left a message.

“Dominic...it’s Penelope. I just wanted to thank you for an amazing dinner.”

Serving HIM continues in Vol. 4, release June 8th.

Acknowledgement

First, we would like to thank all of our readers. Without you, our books would not exist. We truly appreciate each and every one of you.

A big “thanks” goes out to all the Facebook fans, street team, beta readers, and advanced reviewers. You are a HUGE part of the success of the series.

We have to thank our PA, Shannon Hunt. Without you our lives would be a complete and utter mess. Also a big thank you goes out to our editor Lynette and our wonderful cover designer, Sinisa. You make our ideas and writing look so good.

About The Authors

1. MS Parker

M. S. Parker is a USA Today Bestselling author and the author of the Erotic Romance series, Club Privè and Chasing Perfection.

Living in Southern California, she enjoys sitting by the pool with her laptop writing on her next spicy romance.

Growing up all she wanted to be was a dancer, actor or author. So far only the latter has come true but M. S. Parker hasn't retired her dancing shoes just yet. She is still waiting for the call for her to appear on Dancing With The Stars.

When M. S. isn't writing, she can usually be found reading– oops, scratch that! She is always writing.

2. Cassie Wild

Cassie Wild loves romance. Every since she was eight years old she's been reading every romance novel she could get her hands on, always dreaming of writing her own romance novels.

When MS Parker approached her about co-authoring the Serving HIM series, it didn't take Cassie many seconds to say a big yes!!

Serving HIM is only the beginning to the collaboration between MS Parker and Cassie Wild. Another series is already in the planning stages.

Made in the USA
Lexington, KY
17 August 2015